Battletown Tales 1 Rocks, Rats, & Role Models

Battletown Tales 1 Rocks, Rats, & Role Models

Nobutaro Masai

CONTENTS

Battletown Tales 1 Rocks, Rats, & Role Models, and it's respective logos are trademarks of Calen P. Nobutaro Masai in the U.S.A. and other countries.

ISBN: 9781735094137

Cover Art and Illustrations: Overlord (@overload_th)
Editing: Rosalind Sterling

First Printing, paperback edition March 2025
Printed in USA

Acknowledgements

I would like to thank my beautiful fiancé, Brittany, for reading every chapter of this story as it was written and for her love and support while writing this book. I would also like to express my heartfelt gratitude to Elizabeth Cowan, Tasheeta Boyd, Michele Skipper, and Anna Sanders for beta reading this story and sharing their thoughts and insight which helped me tremendously. I want to give a shout-out to Rosalind Sterling who provided amazing editorial assessments that helped me restructure this story. All of the beautiful art in this book was created by the talented Overlord, and I'm so thankful for this opportunity to work together again with this amazing artist.

Glossary

- Battletown Elementary- The local elementary school in Battletown for pre-k through 5th grade. It's located deep underground in the rocky caverns underneath Battletown High and Battletown Middle school.
- Blurf- A profane term meant to strongly curse an undesirable person, place, event, or situation.
- Brickbuster's Cereal- A popular brand of cereal in Zoofria made from grains with a hardness similar to bricks. Their mascot, Bricky, is a sentient brick who is constantly foiling the schemes of the Breakfast Bandits who constantly plot to steal breakfast away from children.
- Brilocks- The official currency of Battletown/all of Zoofria. They are made of ziglinite infused with blood. They are created using a secret technique that only a select few know.
- Dardak- The capital of the monster realm. Covered in a dense layer of darkness, it's the birthplace of all creatures of the night banished from the mortal realm.
- Decree of Brutality- An official law created by the Founding Fathers of Battletown over 3000 years ago to end thoughtless death/murder. It states that the right to rule/subjugate others belongs to those who prevail in a

conflict. Those in power can subjugate others to their will; however, murder is strictly prohibited. Those guilty of murder are marked for death and forfeit all protections granted by this decree. Those marked for death can be killed consequence-free.
- Den of the Defeated- The spiritual realm that Sidven believe they will go to if they are permanently defeated in battle. It's filled with all of the souls killed in battle who now spend all of eternity roaming endlessly with an all-consuming hunger.
- Drux- A unit of measurement equal to 15.6 inches.
- Kadrux- A unit of measurement equal to 5,000 drux. Also equivalent to 78,000 inches.
- Kearce Stadium- The boxing stadium that Alex's older sister, Noel, fights at every night. A boxer's wages are determined by four things: the number of fights they participate in, if they were victorious, their popularity with the crowd, and the sale of their merchandise.
- Rumble bees- Menacing bees that are the size of a child. They hunt prey, ranging from small beasts to large creatures, and use the blood of the living creatures they hunt to make mud nests to dwell in.
- Sidvan/Sidven- The most common race of people residing in Zoofria. They tend to be taller and more muscular than common humans due to a powerful bloodline passed down from their forefathers who migrated from the monster realm.
- Yosmin- A unit of time equivalent to 100 zins (100 seconds).

- Ziglinite- A hard type of rock found in Zoofria with an equivalent hardness to quartz. It first appeared when the Founding Fathers first crossed over to the mortal realm 3,000 years ago. It's a clear stone with the ability to absorb other substances and turn into a matching color. It's most often transformed into brilocks, the official currency of Zoofria.
- Zin- A unit of time equal to 1 second.
- Zoofria- The nation that Battletown resides in.

Prologue

In the land of the north lies the country of Zoofria. Upon this rocky terrain over three thousand years ago, a dark portal opened up, giving way for a distinct group of people. They stood taller than the lankiest of humans with more muscular body types and deep, menacing looks within their eyes. Folks say that these people, referred to as Sidven, were creatures of darkness who forsook the shadows as they migrated from Dardak, the realm of monsters, to make a new life for themselves among the creatures of light.

But civilized life amongst the mortals was vastly different from the barbaric realm of darkness. While some mortals had an equal thirst for bloodshed and conflict, most preferred diplomacy over brutal fights to the death. This put Sidvenkind at odds with other nations and, most frequently, with themselves. To put an end to unnecessary bloodshed, the Forefathers of Zoofria created the Decree of Brutality to limit their violent tendencies while also establishing governance through strength and unyielding determination. Over the millenniums, the savage natures of the Sidven simmered down within most of Zoofria. Their bodies adapted builds similar to those of the humans inhabiting the world, with the former fiery spirit of old carried only by a small handful of Sidven.

Despite the civility seeping within the nation, real monsters still lurked deep within the shadows of the country. Forgotten after many generations and lying in wait to cause chaos within the land of mortals.

This is a tale of a monster that broke free from bondage and the brave forces that banded together to face it. Remember, bravery comes not from fearlessness in the presence of evil, but from the willingness to fight back resolutely despite *having* fear. Because evil only prospers when those of sound morals refuse to confront it. So, to those trapped by fear, doubt, or shame in the face of adversity, keep one thing in mind: be bold when combating wickedness, because malice will always fade like shadows when battling the light of the virtuous.

Chapter 1- My Hero

"Alright, students! It's time to practice what you've learned!" A voice bellowed through a blood-red half-demon mask. Its speaker was clad in ancient samurai armor gleaming a vibrant crimson and gold. Hanging from his right hip was a katana within a lustrous sheath.

He stood in a small, tidy classroom filled with beautiful artwork. The walls were covered in scrolls and canvases portraying ancient warriors, terrifying beasts of old, and women who were the definition of breathtaking. Yet despite all of the intricate, eye-catching objects in the room, what currently garnered the most attention was the clear rock he held within his hands.

"Breaking rocks with only your bare hands is not just a test of strength, but also a test of your strength of mind." His crimson eyes gleamed as he spoke passionately to the third graders before him, holding the crystalized slab of ziglinite bigger than his head. "Stones have a strong will, and yours must be stronger if you're to crush it. Gather every ounce of resolve within your fingertips and press into the rock with every fiber of your being until it breaks."

Every child quietly paid close attention to their shimmering teacher's instructions.

"Not an easy feat to master, but it's important that you learn this. If you can't surpass the will of a single rock, then what hope will you all have against the powers you will face outside these walls? You all must be strong enough to stand up against the forces that will oppose you, or you all will be eaten alive!" he yelled as he closed his fingers. With a loud crack, his rock instantly crumbled into a fine dust around him. He clicked his tongue at the mess before him, and after he blew air at the pile, it rose off the ground and flew into the trash can right next to his wooden desk.

His twelve bright-eyed students applauded briefly with loud cheers, only to simmer down after their instructor motioned for them to be silent. "I also expect you all to clean up after yourselves once your rocks are broken. Every warrior must be neat and well-kept because a disciplined warrior is a formidable force to reckon with. Now pick up your rocks and show me the strength of your will!"

With eager eyes, they each swiftly grabbed a fist-sized stone from their desktops. Without hesitating, their faces became red, their loud grunts filling the air as they tried to crush their rocks using only the strength of their hands. Loud cracks reverberated as several students successfully shattered their rocks.

"Excellent job, class!" their instructor exclaimed joyfully while walking over to one student. This pupil wore a pink

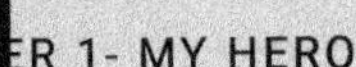

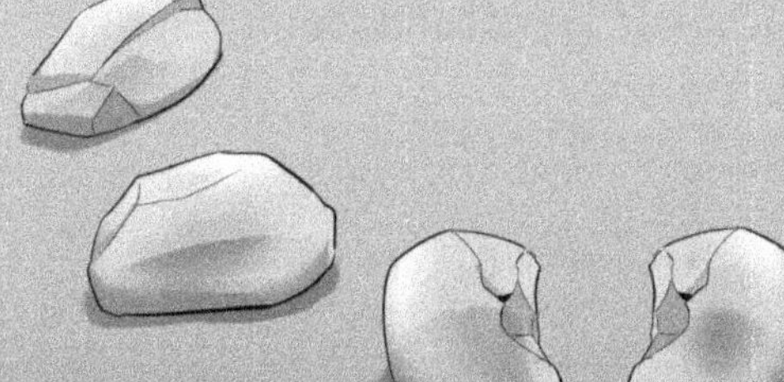
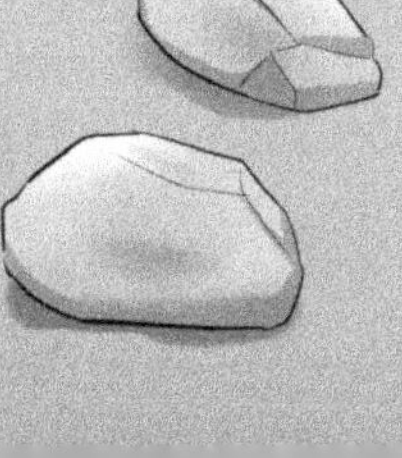

headband and was the first to break her rock into smaller pieces. "Good job, Alex! Your two-handed technique looks great! With a little more work, you'll be able to break rocks with one hand like this," he said after grabbing a rock from the pile on her desk and crushing it into a fine powder with a quick hand movement.

"Thanks, Mr. Striker!" Alex said with a huge smile. She brushed the dirt off her gloved hands nonchalantly before picking up another rock. "Noel has been helping me practice. She said that we can bake some Blood-Red Velvet Cupcakes together over the weekend if I can crush my rocks into fine gravel."

Mr. Striker gave Alex a sticker with a smiling rock that said, "'You rock!'"

"Then keep up the good work, Alex, and I expect you to bring me back a cupcake next week," he said approvingly with Alex giving him a thumbs up in return. Mr. Striker turned his attention to a light brown-skinned girl with an extra-long chestnut ponytail who was sitting next to Alex. Sweat beaded on her face as she barely put a crack on her rock.

"That's a good start, Sara!" Mr. Striker said warmly. "Remember to use those fingers when smashing that rock. A strong grip is vital both in and out of battle."

"Yes, sir, Mr Striker!" Sara grunted while continuing to squeeze her rock, but it slid slightly within her grasp. "If only I hadn't put on my mountain berry hand lotion before this, then my fingers wouldn't be so-"

A frustrated scream interrupted the girl, but Sara only rolled her eyes and muttered, "Rat Face is at it again."

Mr. Striker turned his attention to the student sitting behind Alex and Sara: pale-skinned boy with an unsavory smell and rat-like teeth.

This student was known as Ricky. His face was beet-red with the veins on his forehead visible and throbbing. He had long given up on trying to break his rock with his hands and was now repeatedly banging his rock against his desk with his lips snarled. "Stupid rock! Why won't you break already!" he screamed as his desk, already covered with various markings, received new scrapes with every strike. Several of the other students snickered as he struggled, which only caused him to slam his rock with increased intensity.

Mr. Striker shook his head before clicking his tongue. He grabbed Ricky's hands and effortlessly immobilized them over his head. "That's incorrect, Ricky. This activity is meant to strengthen your hands and will for combat. Every warrior needs a strong grip, a cool head, and boundless inner strength for any trial they may face."

"This is pointless! No one needs that strong of a grip to kill someone! There are plenty of easier ways to take the life of your enemies!" Ricky yelled before breaking from Mr. Striker's grip and hurling his rock at Alex. It sped towards her with impressive speed, but with a nimble head turn, she easily dodged the projectile.

"Ricky, what are you doing? You can't hit me with those skinny arms!" She giggled playfully as Sara gave her a high-five.

"You'd have to get a lot stronger before you could ever leave a mark on me!"

"Shut up! You're so annoying, Alex!" Ricky screamed while picking up the other rocks on his desk and throwing them at Alex, who continued to dodge them effortlessly. "One solid hit could end you!"

"Ricky, just knock it off already," Sara said sharply while glaring at him. "You're only making yourself look bad."

"I said shut up!" Ricky hollered as he threw a rock at Sara. With a flick of her head, Sara's ponytail flew around and batted the rock right back at Ricky, hitting him squarely in the right cheek.

"Owww!" he screamed with tears running down his face as he shot a hate-filled glare at Sara, only for her to return it with matching intensity. "I'll make you two pay for this!" he yelled as he jumped up from his desk and opened his palms, two rats suddenly appearing in his hands.

Alex and Sara jumped up from their desks with determined expressions, eyes trained solely on Ricky as they struck their fighting poses.

The other nine students watched with anticipation from their desks, waiting to see a brawl break out between the three.

The soft *swing* of Mr. Striker unsheathing his katana made all twelve third graders freeze. The glimmering crimson blade radiated fierce energy which sent shivers up every student's spine. The other nine students glanced back down at their desks and grabbed their rocks while squeezing furiously. Alex,

Sara, and Ricky, with tense muscles, slowly turned to face their more-than-unhappy teacher.

"Ricky, you have not only deliberately disobeyed me, but you also tried to harm your classmates. Not to mention you brought vermin into my classroom when you know full well how I feel about keeping my classroom clean. What do you have to say?" he said calmly, the crimson point of his sword resting underneath the boy's chin. Ricky's eyes widened in horror as his face became as white as cotton.

"I'm...sorry. It won't happen again, sir," Ricky managed to say in barely a whisper.

"Good. Remember, Ricky, a good warrior always keeps a cool head, especially in a heated situation. Staying calm can often mean the difference between life and death on the battlefield. Now put away your rats and take a seat before I decide to use the concrete slabs," he said with a low tone and pointed glare. His blade pointed to a wooden kneeling board and several slabs of concrete in the corner of the room.

"Yes, sir," Ricky said after Mr. Striker sheathed his sword. Ricky sighed deeply before snapping his palms shut. His rats disappeared in a blink, and with trembling movements, he silently took his seat. Mr. Striker then turned towards Alex and Sara.

"I have no problem with you two defending yourselves. However, I must remind you both that Ricky is in the same group as you two during assignments in my class, and as such, you three must find a way to work together."

"Come on, Mr. Striker!" Sara complained. "Ricky is such a creep. He leaves nasty rat hairs all over our desks, and he always chews up pencils with his pointed buck teeth. Plus, he smells disgusting. Alex and I don't want to work with him."

"His rats are gross," Alex chimed in. "And Ricky doesn't like working with us anyway."

"Regardless of those things, you may often find yourselves having to work with others with whom you don't see eye to eye. I'm not saying you need to become their best friend, but you have to be at least able to work with them at the bare minimum. He is a part of your group. That makes him important, so you must protect him just like you would protect a comrade in battle. Do you both understand me?"

They both stared deeply into his uncompromising red pupils for a moment before resigning with a sigh.

"Fine," they both muttered before sitting back down in their seats. Both the girls and Ricky refused to look at each other and quickly turned their attention to Mr. Striker who marched back to the front of the classroom.

"Alright, class, now that we've finished crushing rocks with our hands, it's time for our next assignment. I need everyone to clear the rocks off their desks."

"Do we get to practice cave diving?!" Alex asked excitedly.

"No, that'll be next week, Alex," Mr. Striker said with a chuckle before continuing. "This is an assignment that I hold dear to my heart, students. One that will test your innermost being and make you question who you really are."

"That sounds lame," Ricky retorted under his breath, ignoring the glares of the other students. Mr. Striker paused for a moment. His eyes trained on Ricky thoughtfully before shifting to the rest of the class.

"I need everyone to pull out their pens and paper and get into groups of three. We are going to be writing an important essay."

Groans resonated throughout the class as the children cleared their desks and put them together into their predetermined groups. They reluctantly pulled out the necessary supplies from within before returning their attention to Mr. Striker.

"I want everyone to write about their personal hero. It can be about a famous celebrity, a family member, or even someone who was there for you when you needed them. I want a full page written by the end of the day. You may start now, and feel free to talk about it with your desk mates."

The students sighed but began speaking to each other in hushed voices while scribbling down their thoughts.

"Hey, Sara," Alex asked in a low tone, "who are you writing about?"

"I was thinking about writing about Bricky from Brickbuster's Cereal," she giggled gleefully. "I love that he defeats the evil Breakfast Bandits and delivers his rock-hard cereal to everyone, but ..." Her eyes softened as a warm smile spread across her face. "I'm going to write about my dad. He's a police officer who catches bad guys. He even caught Ralphy the Rat Burglar who robbed several banks here in town. Being super sneaky,

Ralphy escaped every other cop, but he couldn't give Dad the slip. My dad caught him without breaking a sweat and had him locked up in jail. He even returned every last brilock that Ralphy stole back to the banks."

"That's insane!" Alex exclaimed. "Your dad is like a real life Bricky!"

"I know," Sara said with a proud smile. "Who are you writing about, Alex?"

"Oh, I'm writing about my sister, Noel," Alex said excitedly while scribbling on her paper furiously. "She's my hero! She was there for me the day the lights went out on our street after that bad hurricane, and after our mom left to go on her really long vacation three months ago. She even began boxing every night so that we could afford cupcakes, juice boxes, and prime ribs. No matter what, my sister is always there for me, and no one can stop her."

"Oh please, your sister is not all that great," Ricky muttered from across his desk while chewing on his pencil. After taking the pencil out of his mouth, he quickly sketched something on his paper. "She's only strong because **the Evil One** kissed her when she was a baby. There's nothing special about her at all."

Alex set her pencil down. Her fist clenched as her narrowed eyes rose from her paper to meet Ricky's gaze. "Don't you dare talk about my sister that way, Ricky!"

"Yeah, no one invited you into our personal conversation, Rat Face, so butt out!" Sara yelled.

"Actually, I'm a part of this group, so yeah, I'm free to join any discussion you two have here," he said before turning his attention back to Alex. "Your sister is lame, almost as lame as Sara's loser dad."

"You want to go, Ricky?!" Sara started to rise from the table but she jolted to a stop when Mr. Striker clicked his tongue. With jerky movements, she turned her head to see her instructor gazing in her direction. His blazing eyes scorched her soul while his hand gripped his katana's hilt. Sara gulped and sat back down in her seat. When Mr. Striker released his hold on his blade, she sighed with relief. "I mean...what's your problem, Ricky?" she asked in a hushed voice after taking one last shaky glance at Mr. Striker.

"My problem is I want a turn to speak, Sara," Ricky said with a wicked smile as he showed his paper, which had the rather well-drawn image of some hideous, humanoid creature wearing a welder's mask over his face and carrying a giant spiked stone mace. Several other kids in class gasped when they saw Ricky's paper. Even Mr. Striker gave a slight look of disapproval at Ricky's drawing but chose to remain silent. "For my essay, I will be writing about Jarg the Devourer. He's way stronger than your heroes combined."

"Who's Jarg?" Alex asked with an uneasy feeling creeping inside her. Only one thing ever put a twinkle in Ricky's eyes, and that was his fascination with the night. It wasn't the darkness that caught his interest, but rather the dangerous creatures that dwelled within the cloak of shadows. Ricky religiously studied such monsters until the late hours of the night and the more destructive, the better. Such topics were not things that

Alex was fond of, as the thought of violent creatures bent on death and destruction deeply frightened her.

"Just some myth, Alex," Sara muttered with a dismissive tone, feeling her shivering bestie tightly clamping onto her waist. She held Alex's quivering hand and gave her a reaffirming smile. "I wouldn't waste my time on anything Ricky says. He's all talk, and nothing he says means anything."

Alex took a deep breath as the warmth from Sara's hand filled her with a kind of courage. Slowly, she returned the smile while tightly squeezing Sara's hand as her shaking ceased.

"Jarg is no myth, Sara," Ricky retorted adamantly. "He's killed countless people effortlessly, paralyzing them with his red glare and feasting on their souls. Now, that is cool!"

"Ricky," Sara said with a frown and both arms crossed over her chest. "Jarg is a murderer. There is nothing cool or heroic about that monster."

"Poor, naïve Sara," Ricky said with a mock sympathetic shake of his head. "Those with the power to kill are the ones with the power to do whatever they want. That is what makes Jarg cool."

"Please, Noel could easily beat Jarg!" Alex exclaimed passionately. "He sounds like nothing more than a meanie. I bet even Sara and I could take him."

"Really?" An eager look appeared in Ricky's eyes as a crooked smile stretched over his face. "Then why don't you prove it?"

"Prove what?" Alex asked with a confused expression.

"Prove that you two can defeat Jarg."

"How would we do that?" Alex asked while scratching her head. "He's just a make-believe monster, and my sister told me that imaginary monsters are nothing compared to the monsters we have in real life."

"What if I told you that your sister was wrong? What if I told you that Jarg was real?" Ricky asked with zeal while slowly leaning forward. His palm opened, and a chubby, brown rat appeared in his hand. "Would you still have the courage to follow through with what you said?" he asked before closing his palm and causing the rat to disappear.

Alex and Sara turned to look at each other for a moment before returning their focus to Ricky.

"Tell us more, Ricky." Alex spoke with a hushed, yet firm, tone.

"Gladly..." Ricky said enthusiastically before his face tensed at the sound of a tongue clicking. He glanced up at Mr. Striker crossing his arms and quickly shifted his eyes toward his desk as he spoke in a whisper. "We need to work on these papers right now. Mr Striker is giving us the evil eye again. Meet me in the spider's web during recess, and I'll tell you everything."

Chapter 2- Unexpected Ambush

After the class bell rang, the twelve children dashed towards the exit but not before their armored instructor uttered a few final remarks. "Remember class you need to have your hero essays turned in by the end of the day. Please be careful in the caverns today. Another colony of rumble bees has invaded Battletown Elementary and several three-headed chickens have been spotted in the caverns lately. I don't want to see any of you getting carried away by insects just as big as you or gobbled up by those giant, acid-spewing birds, so travel in groups at all times and don't dilly-dally. Also, stay off the Crimson Path."

"Why's that, Mr. Striker?" Sara asked. "I heard some older students say that it's a shortcut through the underground caverns."

"It is a perilous one filled with dangerous creatures that make a swarm of rumble bees look harmless." Mr. Striker said calmly but with a serious look in his ruby-colored eyes. "I know several of you may be tempted to take a shortcut to more quickly navigate through this treacherous cavern, but even that is not worth losing life or limb to the dark creatures lurking within that cursed walkway. Am I understood?"

"Sure thing, Mr. Striker!" Alex exclaimed enthusiastically as she jumped out of her seat and landed on her feet with a thud.

Mr. Striker's eyes crinkled, suggesting a small smile was hiding behind the gleaming red demon mouth mask he wore. "Excellent! You all are excused!"

The children quickly exited Mr. Striker's room in a neat and orderly fashion before dispersing into the outside rocky caverns. The air was musty with very little circulation. The only lighting came from the small but resilient flames blazing on the torches against the walls. Eleven of the twelve kids giggled with glee as they dashed down the well-trodden path towards their most favorite time of the day: recess!

"I can't wait once we make it to high school," Alex said as she glanced towards the rocky ceiling while running. "It'll be great taking classes above ground level, smelling fresh air and seeing sunlight during the day."

"Me too, Alex! I can't wait to feel the sunshine! This dim lighting doesn't do my hair justice. Look what the shadows are doing to it. Whose bright idea was it to put Battletown Elementary deep underground anyway?" she whined as she picked up her ponytail and held it in front of Alex's face. "My hair is losing the shine from my mountain berry shampoo."

"Are you sure?" Alex asked while squinting her eyes. "Your hair is still shinier and softer than everyone else's hair in class."

"It'd be even shinier if we could get some blurfing sun down here. I wish we could just make a giant hole in the ceiling to let some in," Sara grumbled with a slight pout before her face became serious. "Are you for real about meeting up with Ricky?"

"You better believe it, Sara!" Alex exclaimed while clenching her fist. "He said my sister was lame and that Jarg is stronger than her. I can't let that slide. Where is he, anyway? I don't see him anywhere," she said while looking around but seeing no one other than Sara close by.

"He probably took cheater's lane to get to the spider's web," Sara said. "You know how badly he hates exercising, especially using the monkey bars. He shirks off every chance he gets, the lazy little louse."

"If only he loved exercise as much as he loved talking about monsters. I'll never understand what his problem is," Alex said as she and the other kids reached the end of the path with only a rocky cliff before them. Surrounding the drop was a deep hole that stretched for approximately one hundred drux and was rumored to be bottomless. Every kid who ever fell in was never seen or heard from again. Some say that the fallen are still falling to this day, while others claim that they end up trapped in eternal darkness, or worse...the Den of the Defeated. The remaining elementary students decided unanimously to just not fall in the hole so that they would never have to find out.

On the other side of this gaping hole was the vast mass of land where the children went every day for recess. Merry-go-rounds, slides, swings, wooden fortresses, and all of the equipment that a small child could desire covered the area. However, only a pair of monkey bars bridged the gap from where Alex and the other children stood. Without hesitating, the children grabbed a hold and began making their way across the chasm, one monkey bar at a time.

"Sara, check this out!" Alex exclaimed. With the help of her grippy gloves, she swung effortlessly from bar to bar and wildly dashed her legs in the air. "I'm running on air!"

Sara, who was matching Alex's pace while sprinting across the top of the bars, laughed. "Nice! You're almost as fast as me in the air!"

"I can still go faster!" Alex grunted as she quickened her pace, her face brimming with determination.

Suddenly a menacing buzz filled the air. Both girls looked back to see two black and yellow rumble bees approaching quickly from behind. Their red eyes locked onto the two girls as the insects zoomed towards them. With loud cracks, they pounded all six of their clenched fists together; their black stingers, sharp enough to pierce stones, were pointed directly at the girls.

"You're going to have to!" Sara exclaimed, her eyes narrowing as she sped up. The sound of her feet clanging as they struck the monkey bars with increased haste resonated. Yet despite her best efforts, the buzzing only grew louder. "Because those bugs aren't going to leave us alone!"

"These rumble bees look hungry!" Alex yelled. "Do you think we can interest them in the cookies I baked this morning?"

"Not a chance, Alex! Rumble bees only hunt live prey, and unfortunately, third graders are on the menu! At this rate, they're going to catch us before we make it to the recess zone!"

"Blurf! And I worked really hard baking them this morning too," Alex whined. She continued to furiously swing from bar to bar. Sweat was now pouring down her face as her breathing was heavy. Sara, meanwhile, was dashing across the monkey bars while pumping her arms, her ponytail swishing behind her. Taking several deep, rhythmic breaths, she appeared mostly unfazed by their pursuers, only wrinkling her nose with a frown at the strong scent of blood reeking from the flying insects.

"Didn't you make those specifically for your sister?" Sara asked casually.

"Yeah...but I want to bake things that every creature can enjoy, even the ruthless rumble bees."

"Bestie," Sara said with a half-amused half-serious expression. "Those flying bugs are here only to enjoy one thing and it's definitely not the cookies in your pocket."

"If cookies won't work, then that leaves us only one option. We'll have to deal with these two pests using other means." Alex grunted as she swung hard to the side with an incredible flip and landed next to Sara on top of the monkey bars. Her eyes brimmed with fierce determination as she reached into her pocket. "I hope Ricky isn't too peeved about us being late, but Noel told me that it's better to arrive late than dead."

She pulled out a rock from her pocket, and with a mighty throw, hurled it at one of the rumble bees. With a loud crack,

it hit the first bee in the face. With a screech, it swerved away from the girls in a daze.

The second bee flew straight towards Sara with six fists raised, but she swiftly turned her head. With a loud crack, her ponytail whipped the bee. It gave a pained cry, but before it could respond, Sara kept relentlessly smacking the bee with her ponytail in a frenzy of vicious blows before finally flicking her head down, and swatting the rumble bee down into the bottomless hole below them.

"Nice one, Sara!" Alex exclaimed as she held out her hand to give Sara a high-five. But before Sara could respond, Alex felt a strong force collide into her. In the blink of an eye, she found herself dangling in the air, held in the firm grasp of the first rumble bee. Alex looked around curiously while the insect pulled her higher toward the ceiling.

"You're a tough one, aren't you?" Alex asked with a ferocious smile as she reached up and grabbed the rumble bee's fist with her free hand. "Unfortunately for you, I spent an entire class breaking things harder than your hand!" she exclaimed as she squeezed the insect's hand until its exoskeleton cracked. The rumble bee flew haphazardly, crying in intense pain, but Alex wasn't done. She quickly pulled herself up until she was sitting atop the creature, and with a swift movement, ripped the bees wings off.

"Now, let's see if I can do it today!" Alex exclaimed as she planted her feet on the insect.

The flailing rumble bee fell into the bottomless pit, but not before Alex leaped off the insect while executing a double spiral backflip as she hurtled upwards by several drux. Her chin-length black hair flapped wildly as she shot up in the air. Her hand reached out as high as she could, trying to touch the jagged rocky ceiling. Yet as her hand was a fingertip away, she found herself plummeting towards the bottomless pit down below.

"I was so close," Alex muttered as a pair of airborne, light brown-skinned hands broke her fall by grabbing ahold of hers.

"You're so reckless, Alex!" Sara said with a laugh while hovering in the air, thanks to her chestnut-colored, extra-long ponytail whirling above her head like a helicopter propeller. "What would you do without me?"

"Probably fall to my death." Alex giggled with a big smile on her face as she dangled her feet in the air playfully. "But I almost reached the top."

"You're always trying to touch the ceiling, even when there is a whole swarm of rumble bees chasing after us," Sara said with a mischievous look in her eyes. "You got a crush on it or something?"

"Hardly!" Alex laughed giddily before returning her gaze to the ceiling. A tender, yet determined, look filled her eyes.

"My sister says only the best can reach the top, and one day I will reach it!" she exclaimed as Sara lowered her to the monkey bars with a clang. Alex peered ahead and saw the spider's web looming ominously above the rest of the rusty and completely unsupervised playground equipment. Their rambunctious classmates were already running rampant throughout the dimly lit area with fire in their eyes and sugar in their bellies. The sound of their heavy steps resembled those of wild beasts battling for dominance. Their loud, giddy shrieks echoed off the cavern walls, which strongly smelled of blood, sweat, and boogers. The jagged playground equipment trembled and creaked under the constant bombardment of brutally bouncy boys and greatly galloping girls, but stubbornly stood strong.

"We're missing out on all of the fun!" Alex exclaimed as she quickly sprinted down the monkey bars. "Come on, Sara! We need to hurry up and talk to Ricky so that we can enjoy the rest of recess!"

"I'm coming," Sara exclaimed with an uncertain expression on her face as she landed and followed after Alex. "But I fear Ricky will be more problematic than an angry horde of rumble bees," she muttered under her breath as they approached the recess area.

Chapter 3- Playground Shenanigans

"Took you two long enough to get here," Ricky grumbled as he saw Alex and Sara approach him inside the spider's web. He sat on one of the lower bars; his fingers intertwined as a rat scurried from one arm to the other. The small creature squeaked happily, but could barely be heard over the loud racket of the other nine children screaming as they played. "I was starting to think that you both flaked out on me. I don't know why you two still bother taking the monkey bars to get here when there is the short tunnel I made that directly leads to the recess zone."

"Because we don't want to take cheater's lane to get here. Also, those tunnels are tight, damp, and terrible for my hair," Sara muttered with a slightly whiny tone before her expression hardened. "Now, what did you want to tell us, Ricky?"

Ricky's rat dashed up to his shoulder and crawled up his neck until it perched right on top of his messy hair. With a big smile and bright eyes, he stood up from the bar and walked towards the two girls.

"Something that will go down in history," Ricky said with a smug smile as he addressed the other children on the playground. "Everyone gather around! I have something to show you all that will shake you to your cores."

The other nine children curiously circled around the outside of the spider's web. With amazing dexterity, Ricky made several hand gestures and chanted an unknown language rhythmically in a low tone.

"Ricky, what are you doing?" Alex asked with a sinking feeling in her gut.

"I'm going to summon Jarg," Ricky said proudly as all of the other kids in the recess zone instantly froze at the sound of Jarg's name. Their eyes widened and their legs trembled. With terrified screams, they ran away and hid behind the playground equipment. Cautiously, they peeked at Ricky with tense expressions as Ricky continued to chant.

"Why does Ricky have to do this weird song and dance routine to summon Jarg?" Alex wondered with a perplexed look. "Is Jarg a big fan of musicals or something?"

"This isn't a dance, Alex. It's a ritual, and I'm doing it because Jarg is a monster among monsters," Ricky said with a gleam in his eyes. The rat on Ricky's head squeaked excitedly as it stood on its hind legs and began waving its front legs wildly in the air as Ricky continued to speak. "He's an unstoppable killing force who gets stronger by consuming others, and summoning him requires a little more umph. The strength of hundreds of thousands of people flows within his black blood, and that power is mine to control. Now arise, Jarg!"

He reached into his pocket and pulled out a chunk of bitter-smelling cheese much to everyone's confusion.

Why does Ricky keep cheese in his pocket? Alex asked herself as she scratched her head while Ricky raised his arms dramatically and dropped the cheese. It landed next to his feet with a thud before disappearing with a loud pop as the other children gasped. What took the place of the cheese after appearing out of nowhere was...a huge, chubby, black rat the size of a football.

"Wow...Jarg is a lot smaller than I thought...and smellier," Alex muttered with a baffled look as the chunky rat scurried away. The rat on top of Ricky's head leaped to the ground, chasing after the larger one. The other children came out from behind the playground equipment, their fear turning into anger as they stomped towards Ricky, Alex, and Sara.

"That's because it's not Jarg. It's just a really big rat, like Ricky," Sara said with an unimpressed expression as she grabbed Alex's hand and began pulling her away. "Rat Face is all talk. Let's go, Alex; recess will be over soon."

"Don't walk away, you two!" Ricky yelled; his eyes narrowed and his frown became rigid. "Something may have gone wrong with my summon, but don't get the wrong idea! I know how to bring him into this world and I'm going to prove it!"

"Yeah right, Ricky!" one of the other kids bellowed while approaching with clenched fists. "Just like when you said you'd call forth Batisero the Magical Killer Bat with a whistle?!"

"Or that you had personal connections to the crocodile pirates who terrorize the seas," another kid yelled with arms their crossed.

"What about your claims that you're close with the dark lord, Devas?" a third kid hollered as he pulled up his sleeves and stepped within arm's reach of Ricky.

"All of those things are true!" Ricky screamed as the mob of children drew closer. "I have a special connection with many monsters!"

"Shut up, Rat Face!" a fourth kid yelled as he pushed Ricky down to the ground. "All you do is talk about monsters and lie about how you can control them! We're sick of your phony monster talk! Cut it out or we're going to—"

"Try it and I'll make you suffer, meathead!" Ricky screamed; his lips unfurled into a snarl, revealing his pointed teeth. He opened his palms, but they were quickly pinned down by several of the other students.

"I'll have Jarg break every bone in your body before he—" A foot rammed into his side with incredible force, cutting off his yell with a gasp.

"You're nothing but a lying rat!" The fourth kid yelled as he repeatedly kicked Ricky, not fazed by his pained groans. "It's time we show you what we think about monsters here!"

"That's enough!" Alex interrupted as she jumped in between the two and pushed the fourth kid away from Ricky. With a growl, she quickly grabbed the kids pinning down Ricky and hurled them several drux away. "Leave him alone!"

"Butt out, Alex!" Ricky yelled. "I can handle this!"

"No, you can't. You're too weak," Sara said sharply before turning towards the other nine children circled around them. "I'm not fond of Ricky's nonstop blabber about monsters any more than the rest of you, but you all have made your point. Now leave," Sara said with a stern expression before sharply turning her head. Her ponytail cracked loudly, causing the remaining children to flinch with hesitant looks before choosing to turn around and resume playing on the playground.

"Thank goodness! Smacking around all of those kids would have taken the shine out of my hair," Sara said with a sigh before returning her glare to Ricky. "Why do you have to keep going on about monsters, Rat Face? Everyone is getting fed up with it. You need to just drop it and find something else to talk about."

"I will not," Ricky groaned as he slowly sat up. "You have your police officer father and Alex has her older sister. Everyone else is allowed to talk about their heroes openly, so I will talk about mine as well even if they aren't liked by anyone else."

"Ricky," Alex said sympathetically as she helped Ricky back to his feet, "no one else idolizes a murderer."

"That's just because none of you know how cool Jarg is." Ricky scoffed as he brushed off Alex's hands and put his palms together. After uttering a few words, he pulled his hands apart and an old, tattered book appeared in his palms. "I mean, how can you if you've never gotten to truly witness his greatness firsthand?"

"Ricky, what is that?" Alex asked, pointing at the huge book in his hands.

"It's the key to bringing Jarg back. This is the Darshnii, the book of monsters. I found it in my attic back at home. This book details exactly how to perform the ritual to summon any monster, including Jarg. Now, what did I get wrong?" Ricky said with an all-knowing expression as he flipped through the yellow pages. His brows furrowed with his brown eyes looking intently at something that caught his interest. "Oh...so that's why."

"What is it?" Alex asked as she and Sara crept closer, trying to get a peek of the book's content over his shoulder.

"Here, take a look," Ricky said with a smug grin as he handed them the book.

Alex glanced at Sara, who gave her a skeptical look, before Alex grabbed ahold of Ricky's book and flipped through the pages filled with various images of monsters surrounded by piles of text. After a moment, they fell upon Jarg's page. Both of their jaws dropped.

"There's like a kajillion words on this page, and I don't know half of them!" Alex exclaimed, red-faced, with her eyebrows furrowed. She could feel smoke coming from her ears as her brain tried futilely to make sense of the complex terminology and detailed images.

"Yeah, this is a highly advanced-looking ritual," Sara said with a dubious expression before closing the book. "This doesn't look like something you or any other third grader could pull off."

"Don't doubt my abilities, you stupid helicopter girl!" Ricky roared as he snatched the book back from her. "I can totally summon Jarg into this world, and I'll prove it today!"

"Why do you need to throw strawberry jam on a black cup while doing some crazy dance to summon Jarg?" Alex asked after snatching the book back and taking another look inside.

"Oh, that's not strawberry jam, Alex," Ricky said with a sinister smile after yanking it back from Alex. "But that is vital for summoning Jarg since cheese isn't an offering that interests him."

"Right... how exactly are you going to do that?" Sara asked skeptically.

"Hidden deep within these underground caverns is an ancient chamber dating back to the time of our forefathers. Inside is a black circular stone altar covered in old monster runes and adorned with an obsidian horn. I will use it to perform a ritual to bring Jarg back into this world. Then you will have your chance to fight him if you think you two still have what it takes to contend with a merciless murderer."

"Sara and I can take on anything that you throw our way!" Alex exclaimed passionately before Sara quickly put a hand over Alex's mouth and started pulling her away.

"We do not need to justify our strength to you, Ricky," Sara muttered while waving him off. "Alex and I could easily handle anything you can summon. Your monsters are weak and not worth the time of day, just like you. Now, knock off your crazy talk, Rat Face, or I'll show you what happens to those who wind up on the wrong side of my ponytail," she said with a low, menacing tone as her ponytail whizzed rapidly overhead.

Ricky gave both girls a long, piercing glare after closing the Darshnii. He walked away with an irate expression, but not before muttering under his breath ten words in a chilling tone. "I'm going to make you two pay for disrespecting me."

Chapter 4- The Black Altar

After a hino, a giant metal bell shaped like a fist clanged loudly from the ceiling. All of the students looked up with dismay and sighed before slowly making their way back to the monkey bars.

"Looks like recess is over for the day," Alex groaned. "Guess we better make our way to Ruggerritz's room. I hear we'll be continuing our work on building up a tolerance to poisonous things."

"I hope that we don't have to go bathing in the toxic tulip cave again. The fumes are terrible for my hair," Sara moaned as Alex put her arm around her shoulders.

"How about we share some of the cookies I baked this morning to make things better," Alex said with a smile as she reached into her pockets and pulled out a bag of sweet-smelling treats topped with colorful sprinkles.

"I'd like that," Sara said as she eagerly took a sugar cookie from the bag. She took a big bite of her cookie, her ivory teeth sinking through the soft pastry as pure sugary goodness filled her mouth. After munching with an elated expression, she swallowed and sighed contently. "You've gotten a lot better at baking, Alex."

"Thanks!" Alex said, her smile widening after Sara quickly scarfed down the rest of the cookie. "I made plenty extra, so help yourself, bestie. Maybe next time I can make cupcakes."

"I'm surprised you had to bake today. Noel should've been baking for you. I feel like she's been spending less time with you since becoming a boxer."

"I don't mind, I love baking goodies," Alex said nonchalantly as she waved off Sara's concerns. "Besides, Noel has an important boxing match with Mac-en-Clobber, so she didn't have time to be in the kitchen today. She said that we'll celebrate tonight after she wins."

"She better have something good planned! She needs to make up for lost time, especially today of all days!" Sara exclaimed, her mouth covered in cookie crumbs as she grabbed another cookie. She was about to bite into it when Alex frantically tugged on her sleeve.

"Look, Sara," Alex said tensely while pointing at the one student not walking with them. Several drux away from the rest of the group, he trudged farther away down the rocky cavern. "Ricky's going somewhere else."

"He's probably going to take cheater's lane to get to class; the little pansy never uses the monkey bars," Sara muttered under her breath without missing a beat. "I can't stand that beady-eyed creep."

"No, look closer," Alex insisted in a hushed whisper as she halted Sara and turned her to fully face Ricky's direction. "Something's not right."

After a closer look, both girls saw Ricky sulking past cheater's lane. He wore a dark expression, his eyes brooding as he marched like he had somewhere to be, only stopping when he stood before a passageway.

It was made of blood-red rocks reeking of iron and covered in various animal footprints. There was no lighting down this path, creating shadows so dense you could almost feel them. Strange noises and growls from ferocious beasts echoed from this path, their sources concealed within the darkness growing thicker the farther one traveled.

Seeming to not care if anyone was watching, he stared into the shadows that covered the path like he was looking for something. After a moment, he stepped onto the Crimson Path and quickly disappeared.

"Wait! That's the Crimson Path!" Alex gasped. "Mr. Striker said that we can't go down there! Why's he going down there?"

"I don't care what he's up to, Alex. Let's just head to class. He's not worth the time of day," Sara said before grabbing ahold of Alex's hand and pulling her towards the monkey bars.

"You might be right, Sara..." Alex muttered passively, but her feet stayed planted on the ground. Her mind wandered back to a time when she had run away from home when she was five years old after her mother forgot her birthday. She wore a frilled pink party dress with a cardboard birthday crown. She sat like a crumpled flower behind Stan's Soda

Shack. With giant tears pouring down her face like a river with a broken dam, she bawled loudly as the day was devoured by the shadows of night. She didn't remember how long she was out there, but what happened next was forever cemented into her mind. Noel appeared before her, wearing a red dress with a black plastic crown adorning her forehead. The single rope braid woven from her bangs flapped loosely over the whirlwind of emotions brewing on her face.

"I've been looking for you all night, Alex," Noel said in nearly a sob as she quickly wrapped her arms around Alex in a rib-cracking bear hug. Before Alex could respond, Noel scooped up Alex and carried her in her arms. "Let's go home."

Alex put her hands on Noel's face, tracing the bags under her sister's eyes that weren't there before. Noel only looked upon her with a gentle warmth while cradling her tenderly.

"Don't ever run away like that again, Alex," Noel said sternly but with the warmth never leaving her brown eyes. "No one should ever run off into the shadows to disappear forever, not even the worst of the worst."

Those words resonated deeply within Alex's mind as Sara kept trying to pull her in the direction of their next class, but she refused to budge.

"Come on, Alex. If we don't get to Mrs. Ruggerritz's class soon, then we'll have to spend time with the poison-spewing petunias for being late."

"We need to go after him, Sara," Alex said firmly as she turned to face her.

Sara's eyes nearly popped out of her head as she stopped with a dumbfounded expression. But after looking deeply into Alex's face, she realized that her bestie was serious.

"You sure about this, Alex?" Sara asked in a slow, controlled tone. "That path is not one that we need to go down; Ricky's not worth the trouble."

"I'm sure," Alex said definitively with hands on both hips. "We may not like him, but no one should disappear alone down a dark path, not even Ricky."

"I'm not sure about this," Sara whispered doubtfully, her lips forming a tight frown as she crossed her arms.

Alex saw the strong disapproval radiating off of Sara, so she met her gaze with an unyielding stare. Her brown eyes bore deeply into Sara's blue pupils with an unwavering strength fueled by a strange feeling welling within her heart. It whispered quietly, yet firmly, that everything would be alright. This message coursed through her like a tide, growing in size and intensity before crashing onto the bank of her being. This wave carried a force strong enough to leave an unshakeable impression that even Sara could detect with her bestie ultimately sighing deeply before responding. "Then I will back you up, Alex. I still think that this is a really bad idea, though."

"Don't worry, Sara. Whether it's rats, rocks, or even Jarg himself, we handle anything that comes our way. And we'll do it together!" Alex said as she grabbed ahold of Sara's hand and nearly dragged her away as she sprinted until they stood in front of the entrance of the Crimson Path. The darkness cloaking the scarlet walkway grinned menacingly at them with vicious growls of many hidden creatures reverberating within the cavern walls. Alex's nose wrinkled in disgust as the scent of spilled plasma and raw flesh filled the air. But she held her breath and mustered all of her courage as she leaped into the shadows with Sara reluctantly following suit.

...

"Alex, do you have any idea which way we need to be going?" Sara asked with an eyebrow raised, not that it could be seen in the thick shadows.

"Not really, but he can't be too much farther away. He only got a small head start on us," Alex said while squinting in the dark. "I wish I could see better in the dark. Noel is a lot better than me at it; she said it takes a lot of practice."

They had been exploring the Crimson Path for a while, but still couldn't find a trace of Ricky anywhere. Every time they felt they were close, they either ran into a wall, tripped over a pothole, or felt the presence of menacing beasts veiled behind the ominous darkness. It felt almost like the shadows were toying with them, guiding their very movements with cold, calculating fingers, and taking sadistic pleasure in seeing them wander aimlessly within their domain.

We will make it through this, Alex thought to herself. Her legs shook with every step as she tightly held onto Sara's hand. Neither's steps wavered as they carefully crept down the Crimson Path with tense movements. "We just need a way to track down Ricky. Sara, do you have any cheese?"

"How about you try calling my name instead?" a snarky voice responded right next to them. Both girls shrieked loudly before the other voice quickly put his hands over their mouths. "Shush you two! Before you attract a whole herd of vicious creatures our way."

"Ricky!!!" both girls yelled while simultaneously smacking his hands off their mouths.

"What are you two doing following after me?" Ricky demanded with an irritated tone. "It's not cool to stalk people, you know."

"You could tell?" Alex asked, the disappointment evident in her tone.

"Alex, I spend most of my time being ignored and overlooked by others. I can tell when someone is excessively observing me. Now, what do you two want with me? You just come all this way to tell me off again?" Ricky grumbled in an annoyed tone.

"No, we're here to bring you back to Mrs. Ruggerritz's class. Now let's get off of this creepy path and go to class, Ricky," Alex declared.

"First of all, even if I actually wanted to do that, do you even know the way back, Alex?"

"Sure," Alex said before pointing behind her. "All we have to do is go that way."

Ricky face-palmed before responding. "Not even close. It's just what I thought. You two are lost and have no idea how to get back."

"Lay off her, Rat Face!" Sara sneered at him. "Like you could do any better."

"I actually have been exploring this hallway a lot recently, and have a great system for navigating the Crimson Path. It seems like you two may even need my help to get back safely."

"That would be great—" Alex said before being interrupted by Ricky.

"But I'll only help you two get back if you come with me to the hidden chamber and witness me summon Jarg first. Deal?"

Both girls were quiet with Alex tightly squeezing Sara's hand before responding.

"Why do you want to summon Jarg so badly?" Alex asked. "He sounds really dangerous."

"He is, and that's why I want to bring him back into this world. Too many Sidven here have such big heads because of their strength. I want them to know how it feels to be weak and helpless in the presence of someone far stronger than them."

"That's mean, though," Alex said.

"Is your sister any different?" Ricky snapped back. "She beats up her opponents to a bloody pulp every night at Kearce Stadium. And Ralph the Rat Burglar was my cousin. Sara's dad arrested him after he caught my cousin trying to get enough money to save our grandmother. Thanks to Sara's dad, my grandmother died a slow and painful death without a single hope that things would get better. How is that any different than what Jarg does?"

"Because Jarg kills others without a reason," Sara said in a huffy tone with both hands on her hips. "My father only goes after criminals and lowlifes who cause trouble."

"And Noel is a boxer. It's her job to beat her opponents in a fistfight," Alex said nonchalantly. "Her foes wouldn't hesitate to pound her into the ground if given the opportunity, so she doesn't give them the chance for victory."

"I'm not interested in hearing either of your excuses," Ricky said with a cavalier tone as he extended an open hand. "Now, do we have a deal?"

After a moment of silently staring at each other, Alex reluctantly grabbed ahold of his hand and shook it firmly, much to Sara's displeasure.

"Alright, Ricky, so where are we going?" Alex muttered before releasing her grip as the skinny, messy-haired boy flashed her a rat-like smile.

"Just follow me," he said before scurrying down the pitch-black pathway. Alex and Sara followed cautiously, freezing only when they heard another loud growl from some nearby creature hidden in the shadows, causing both girls to jump.

"You two afraid some scary creature is going to gobble you up?" Ricky sneered. "Or are you scared to go somewhere when your big sister isn't there to protect you?"

"Alex is braver than you any day of the week," Sara snarled while pressing a finger into his chest. "Unlike you, Alex doesn't flee during monster attacks. Yeah, she may be a bit spooked now, but who can blame her? Monsters only seem scary when you can't see them. Clear away the darkness and there's no creature that we can't face."

"Oh, really? Then prove it," Ricky said nonchalantly, brushing off Sara's finger before stepping onto the Crimson

Path. "If you don't have the strength to keep moving forward on this path, despite hearing a little growling, then how will you fare against what's coming next?"

"When that comes, we'll face it together," Alex exclaimed as she continued to hold Sara's hand.

"We'll see how far that gets you two," Ricky said with an amused smile. He opened his palms as several rats appeared within both before scurrying down his arms, leaping to the ground, and surrounding all three of them.

"Eww!" Sara exclaimed with a disgusted look. "Put those things away, Ricky!"

"Yeah, your rats are gross!" Alex chimed in with Ricky's smug smile widening.

"No can do, because these cute little guys are going to be our key to safely getting to and from here. Rats can navigate in the darkness remarkably well thanks to their whiskers and their excellent sense of hearing and smell." Ricky said with a smug smile while puffing out his chest before pointing up ahead and loudly yelling, "Take us to the altar!" Every rat immediately ran down the stained path, and Ricky scampered after the swarm in mad pursuit. "I hope that you two can keep up with me and the rat squad, otherwise you'll end up lost."

"Keeping up with you won't be a problem, Rat Boy!" Sara smirked before she and Alex effortlessly sprinted and caught up to him. Not wanting to be outdone, Ricky grunted before running at full speed through the twists and turns of the long, winding, unlevel path, but the girls continued to match him tirelessly.

"Yeah, remember, Coach Funmire has us run laps daily around the school on both legs, then on one leg, then on the other leg, and ending with a hand stand around Battletown Elementary. This is easy in comparison," Alex said while noticing Ricky struggling to keep up with his rats, red-faced and heavily gasping for air. "Maybe you should try exercising during PE more, Ricky, instead of trying to lie and cheat your way out of work?"

"Maybe...you should...shut up, Alex!" Ricky bellowed in between pants with Sara driving her fist into his stomach in response. "Ow!...What was...that for!" Ricky groaned after falling to the ground and clutching his abdomen.

"For being mean!" Sara yelled as she and Alex ceased their running with impatient expressions. Only the rats looked upon Ricky with sympathy. "Now, how much farther? We don't have much time before class starts."

"We're at the spot," Ricky muttered as he put a hand on the wall that stood in front of them. He slowly got back on his feet and snapped his fingers. The rats instantly dispersed around them. They could be heard scurrying on the rocky ground before leaping onto the walls and disappearing into the cracks. After a moment, a loud click reverberated as the wall opened up slowly, revealing a secret room with several tall, wooden torches that cracked ominously. A chill ran down Alex and Sara's spines despite the presence of these flames. They walked cautiously into the musty room reeking of iron and decay with wide eyes and open mouths.

"Where are we?" Alex asked while looking around wildly. They stood in a vast hollowed-out space within the cavern. Many crude drawings of various monstrous beasts covered the smooth walls, along with many blood splatters. Portions of the rocky ground were half melted as if someone had been throwing globs of acid around the room. The most frightening was an obsidian altar in the middle of the room, covered with many dry bones and an onyx horn that exuded an air of dominance. In its black metal was engraved an ancient-looking text that Alex and Sara couldn't read, but both girls instinctively feared.

"This is some kind of secret summoning room," Ricky said while walking to the altar. "My rats discovered it recently. I don't know why it's down here, but this altar enhances my summoning ability. Normally, the most I can summon are my rats, but with this, I can summon far stronger creatures!"

Ricky pulled out a small, clear, plastic bag filled with a muddy red liquid from his pocket and held it up for both girls to see.

"Ew, your strawberry jam looks rotten. Did you leave it out too long in the sun?" Alex asked with her eyes narrowed and her lips in a frown. Her nose wrinkled a bit at the sight of the bag with a sinking feeling in the pit of her stomach.

"It's not jam, Alex. Why do you have a blood packet, Ricky?" Sara asked warily.

"Because to summon anything, you need an offering," Ricky said as he tore open the bag and poured its murky contents over the altar. "And to summon a monster like Jarg, you need blood."

After the bag was emptied, Ricky threw it to the ground and linked his fingers together. In a low voice, he began to mutter a strange chant that filled the girls with dread. Alex and Sara couldn't make out the words that he was using, only that they weren't from their native language, but likely from one far older.

"Now depart from the dark abyss and appear by my side, Jarg!" Ricky bellowed as he broke his finger links and threw his hands into the air.

Nothing happened.

"Um, Ricky...is something supposed to be happening now?" Alex said while scratching her head.

"Yes! I poured the pig's blood and recited the chant correctly." Ricky said with a confused expression. "A door from the dark world should have appeared with Jarg emerging through."

"Well, clearly, you did something wrong, and now all three of us are going to be late for class for nothing. Thanks for wasting our time, Rat Boy," Sara grumbled before grabbing Alex's hand. "This has been nothing but a waste of time. Now Mrs. Ruggerritz is going to—" Sara started to say before being interrupted by a loud squawking that pierced the air.

A loud stomping could be heard, and the ground rumbled in sync. All three children turned toward the source of the noise and stared in horror at the enormous creature that stood before them. With dark brown feathers, scaly feet, and six piercing yellow eyes, Alex, Sara, and Ricky found themselves looking up at a giant three-headed chicken, staring down at them hungrily.

Chapter 5- Chuck's Rampage

"Holy Blurf!" Alex exclaimed as the giant three-headed chicken dashed towards her and the others. The middle head lunged towards Alex, but she nimbly cartwheeled out of the way. "Sara, be careful! This chicken is really dangerous!"

"I can see that!" Sara said while swinging her ponytail rapidly overhead, causing her to float off the ground. The right head of the chicken tried pecking Sara, but she zoomed away and flew behind the beast. "We need a plan to beat this thing."

The creature charged her. Alex rolled away from the massive talons and said, "Well, Chuck has three heads. We each should take one out."

"Are you out of your mind! Three-headed chickens are distant relatives of dinosaurs!" Ricky yelled while cowering behind a massive rock within the cavern. "I'm not going anywhere near that killer clucker! You two are on your own!"

"Wow, you're soooo helpful, Ricky. No wonder everyone thinks so highly of you," Sara muttered sarcastically, her body flying haphazardly. Her head jerked to the right, just narrowly avoiding the deadly lunge of the left head. "How about Charles? This overgrown chicky looks like a Charles."

The chicken, apparently not liking either choice for a name, aimed his posterior at Alex and took a deep squat while bearing down heavily. With a series of loud pops, Chuck shot out several enormous green eggs covered with red spots, the size of fire hydrants, in the direction of the tumbling girl with cannonball-like intensity.

"Nope," Alex repeated stubbornly while performing several aerial flips to avoid the incoming eggs. "His name is Chuck, Chuck the Chicken."

Chuck growled viciously after missing Alex three times. Noticing Ricky peeking his head out from behind the rock, Chuck aimed his feathered booty toward the boy and let loose a monstrous explosion that sent a giant chicken egg flying right at him.

"That's great!!!" Ricky screamed as he ducked his head behind the rock that Chuck's egg splatted across, leaving the boulder covered in a slimy, colossal, red egg yolk filled with a green liquid with Ricky making a disgusted face. "Now can you please think of a way to kill this thing?!!!"

Chuck gave a frustrated squawk as he straightened his legs, resuming his chase after Alex, and quickly caught up to her. With massive steps, the monster brought down his talons, trying to squash his prey, but Alex was much too agile.

CHAPTER 5- CHUCK'S RAMPAGE – | 53 |

"Well..." Alex said after cartwheeling on the rocky floor and just narrowly avoiding one of Chuck's scaly talons as it hit the ground. "If Noel was here, I know she could take it out with one punch."

"Well, your sister isn't here!" Ricky yelled. "And none of us are anywhere near as strong as her!"

"I hate to agree with Rat Face over here, but he has a point. None of us are strong enough to punch any of Chuck's heads off. We're going to have to think of something else," Sara muttered unhappily. She whizzed around the air over Chuck. The beast growled viciously as all three heads turned their attention to Sara.

"Oh great," Sara groaned, now jerking wildly with three enraged chicken heads lunging at her with a single-minded intensity. "We need to come up with a plan now! I won't be able to hold off all three of them for too much longer."

What can we do? Alex thought to herself. *We need to find a way to beat Chuck. I'm good at jumping and rolling, Sara can fly, and Ricky can control rats. There has to be something that we can do to turn things around. If only Mr. Striker had taught us how to break things harder than...* That's when her gaze shifted upwards as a crazy idea formed in her head. She cupped her hands over her mouth and called out to Sara.

"I think I have something, but I'll need a lift, Sara!" Alex yelled before raising her arms as high as they would go.

"You got it, Alex! Here I come!" Sara hollered. With a swift motion, she nosedived in a beautiful spiral before reaching out and grabbing ahold of Alex's arms and lifting her friend off the ground. "So, where do you need me to take you?"

Alex grinned. "To the very top."

"You got it, bestie!" Sara hollered, shooting straight upwards towards the cavern's ceiling at her top speed and narrowly avoiding all three of Chuck's heads, until they hovered a few drux below the jagged rocky ceiling. "I think this is your stop!" she yelled as she swung Alex upwards. With a hearty giggle, Alex soared up until she collided with the ceiling. After latching on tightly, she quickly crawled across the misshapen, hard surface.

"Sara, you and Ricky keep Chuck busy underneath for a bit!" Alex exclaimed as she approached a huge slab of black stone protruding from the ceiling, easily two to three times bigger than her, and grabbed ahold of it. "I'm going to make him a surprise!"

"I'll keep him busy for as long as I can!" Sara yelled before turning around and flying underneath Chuck's legs. "Go do your thing, Alex!"

"You two are crazy!" Ricky yelled, his head peeking out slightly from behind his rock. "I'm not going anywhere near that three-headed monster!"

"Come on, Ricky, we could use your help," Alex grunted as she put her arms around the black slab and tried crushing it, but the rock refused to crumble. *Wow, this rock is a lot harder to break than the one in class! I guess I'm going to have to try harder!*

Her face turned red with both hands shaking violently as she channeled 110% of her strength into her arms. The black slab was tenacious, but after a few moments of Alex unyieldingly pressing into it, loud cracks filled the air. Small pebbles fell to the ground as Alex's grip digging into the rock slowly caused more and more cracks to appear around the slab's base.

"I don't care what you two dimwits need! I'm not leaving this spot no matter what!" Ricky declared adamantly with arms crossed until he heard two heavy footsteps stomping loudly behind him. His lips tensed as he turned his head rigidly, only to see all six of Chuck's beady eyes staring down at him hungrily. All three heads struggled and strained furiously to move around the rock and reach Ricky. After a few infuriating moments, Chuck's three heads turned their focus on the boulder blocking their path. The feathered monster made a terrible retching sound like he was trying to cough up a hairball. The scent of sulfur filled the air as sudden realization filled Ricky's eyes.

"Oh blurf! I forgot they shoot acid!" he screamed as all three heads vomited globs of green goo right at him. The rat boy quickly jumped out of the way as the rock behind him took the brunt of the impact. Within moments, the acidic poison had dissolved it down to a puddle.

"Really?!" Ricky exclaimed after landing on all fours. "Why go after me? The girls are much tastier than me!"

Chuck's three heads lunged at Ricky, but he leaped out of the way and quickly scampered away. "Just to make things clear, I'm not doing this for either of you two!" Ricky yelled while Chuck chased after him in hot pursuit. "I'm doing this to stay alive! I have no desire to work together with you girls!"

"You may want to change your mind about that!" Alex groaned, her face beading with sweat while the whole slab shook. "Sara, can you lead Chuck to the spot right below me?"

"I'll see what I can do!" She circled around Chuck until she drew the monster's attention away from Ricky. After all three heads were focused on her, she flew away from the squawking behemoth. It roared loudly and quickly pursued after her. A worried expression covered Sara's face, now not from the giant chicken tailing her, but from the realization of what Alex was planning to do. "Are you going to be okay?"

"Of course, bestie!" Alex exclaimed with a pained smile. "Just be ready to move because any moment I'll be coming d... AAAAAHHHHHHH!!!" she screamed as the black slab broke off into several smaller rocks that plummeted towards the ground.

"Oh blurf!!!" Ricky screamed, noticing with wide eyes the rock quickly gaining velocity during its fall. Wasting no time at all, he sprinted as fast as his little legs would allow away from the impending impact of the descending slab.

"I HOPE YOU'RE READY FOR YOUR SURPRISE, CHUCK!" Alex screamed, clutching onto the highest of the falling rocks as it hurtled downward at an alarming rate. The three-headed behemoth barely had time to look up in shock before several rocks crashed down on it. Chuck let loose a monstrous roar that was instantly muffled when the broken pieces of slab slammed into the ground with a loud crash. A large, billowing cloud of dust reeking of iron filled the room, but Alex's excitement was short-lived. Her eyes widened as a sobering realization dawned upon her.

Oh yeah, I'm still on this rock. This may be how things end. Drat, Noel is going to kill me, Alex thought until she felt a pair of arms around her waist.

"Did you even have a plan for getting off that giant rock after you broke it off the ceiling?" Sara asked with a half-peeved, half-joking look after she pulled Alex off of the falling rock.

"Nope!" Alex said with a smile while playfully dangling her feet as the black slab plummeted downwards. "Thankfully you were here to catch me."

"It would have been nice if someone was there to help me during all of that!" Ricky yelled from behind the fallen rock. He coughed as he fanned the air around him with his free hand. After a few moments, the dust began to settle, revealing the black slab now wedged into the ground with numerous cracks scattered around the flooring. All three of Chuck's motionless heads stuck out from underneath the fallen rock. Their lifeless eyes gazed at the three children as if they were trying to get one last look before departing to the Den of the Defeated.

"Leaving me with that horrible monster was not cool at all, you two!" Ricky complained, taking a quick uneasy glance at Chuck before turning his focus back to the girls. "I could have died!"

"Oh, put a sock in it, Rat Face!" Sara retorted while lowering Alex back onto the shattered remains of the ground before landing herself. "Alex and I still did the most work to deal with Chuck. If it wasn't for us, you would have been chicken feed."

"Please, I easily could have dealt with Chuck...I mean, that chicken monstrosity if I wanted to," Ricky said with a huffy voice while puffing out his chest and strutting across the uneven ground nonchalantly. "I follow the ways of Jarg, and Jarg never fails to catch his prey."

"Please! Fanboying over some stupid killer is not—" Sara started to say before Alex interrupted her by shaking her shoulder.

"Sara, look!" Alex said after pointing to the other side of the room. The black altar and the ten drux area around it had remained completely undamaged by the falling stone. The three children approached it curiously, only stopping when they stepped in what felt like a warm puddle. Their eyes widened in surprise at the green liquid seeping across the ground.

"That's blood!" Alex yelled as she shook the green gunk off of her shoes. "Where did that come from?"

"Obviously from the three-headed chicken, stupid," Ricky muttered, a strange look filling his eyes. Before either girl could say anything, Ricky scooped up a handful of the murky green blood and flicked it on the black altar. Ricky began making a series of bizarre hand gestures with his eyes closed while once more speaking in a low, unfamiliar tongue that filled both girls with immense dread. But this time it was different. The torch light flickered erratically before transforming into ominous obsidian flames. Giant eyeballs with piercing red pupils appeared within the pitch-black fires and stared intently at the kids as a dull, groan-like humming resonated around the altar.

Both girls tensed up; within both of their hearts, they felt an unfamiliar voice pounding fervently. It spoke without words, but got one urgent message across to them instantly: You need to leave, right now!

"Umm...Ricky, I have a really bad feeling about this," Sara said as she felt herself shaking.

Alex felt her body trembling and grabbed ahold of her bestie's hand tightly.

"Yeah, I don't want to do this anymore, either. Let's just get out of here, Ricky," she added.

"Oh, where did all of that courage that you had fighting Chuck go?" Ricky taunted after finishing the last of his hand gestures.

The altar began radiating a putrid aura, reeking of death and decay.

"Does the thought of encountering a real monster now frighten you two?"

"It's not about being scared, Ricky!" Sara yelled. "It's about messing with things that shouldn't be messed with. Nothing about this feels right!"

"Maybe not for you two, but for me, this is everything that I have dreamed of!" Ricky said while smiling darkly. His eyes filled with an evil gleam that sparkled with every sin he could imagine. He turned towards the altar with wicked jubilation as he spoke with a loud voice. "Now arise, Jarg! Come back into this realm to wreak havoc and carnage! Fill the streets with the blood of your victims until they overflow!"

As if on command, the vile presence from the altar grew, like a malignant tumor, until it manifested a small black hole. Alex and Sara had no idea what this opening was, only that what seeped out from it was bone-chilling, gut-wrenching despair like nothing they had ever experienced. Slowly, a towering figure with brown hair resembling a lion's mane and standing approximately seven drux tall emerged from the hole. He wore obsidian clothing with a spiked black and red turtle shell on his back. Over his face was a dark orange welder's mask covered with a large, pitch-black X. Above the eerie red lens of the mask was an obsidian horn sharp enough to effortlessly pierce any living creature. The most menacing of all was the massive spiked, stone mace that Jarg held effortlessly with just one hand. It radiated an ancient kind of evil that terrified both girls beyond measure.

"Alex, we have to get out of here! Now!" Sara yelled while pulling Alex towards the exit, but she wouldn't budge.

"No!" Alex insisted while pulling Sara back towards her. "Ricky is still a part of our group. We can't leave him here with this...evil monster."

"Alex, I couldn't care less about Rat Face Ricky right now. If he wants to dabble with evil forces, then so be it, but you are my friend and I won't let you get caught up in this mess, so let's beat it!"

"Not until Ricky's safe!" Alex yelled as she heard Mr. Striker's words echo in her mind. *He is a part of your group.*

That makes him important, so you must protect him just like you would protect a comrade in battle. "He's a part of our team, Sara, and Mr. Striker said that we need to save him no matter what!"

"Alex, this isn't something that we can save him from!"

It was Ricky's high-pitched, maniacal laughter that interrupted their conversation. "You two must be crazy if you think I'm going anywhere right now! I can finally feel Jarg's overwhelming power firsthand! You two are more than welcome to flee like scared rabbits, but I'm staying here and witnessing Jarg's rampage! Maybe I'll turn him loose on the other kids in our class first! I'd love to hear the sound of their screams as Jarg splatters them all over the ground!"

"We're not going to let you do that, Ricky! We're leaving here and you will be coming with us!" Alex declared boldly before turning towards Jarg with the monster returning her gaze. Her knees quivered and her blood became ice, but despite that, she raised her fists and struck a fighting pose with Sara following suit behind her. "And if we have to defeat that murderous monster, then so be it!"

"I'd like to see you two try!" Ricky yelled before turning his attention back to Jarg. The monster stood still as a statue, quietly observing all three children like a beast keeping careful watch of his prey. Slowly, he turned his head as Ricky pointed at Alex and Sara.

"Jarg!" Ricky bellowed at the top of his voice. "I command you to trounce those two girls!"

Chapter 6- Battle with a Real Monster Part 1

Jarg, with loud, thunderous footsteps, trudged towards the girls. He stared at them like they were mere flies to swat. His gloved hand tightly gripped his mace, the spiked weapon ready to strike down any who stood before it.

Alex's eyes met this monster's gaze as it slowly approached. She felt the urge to run, but couldn't get her legs to move. *This is really bad! I've got to do something or Jarg will splatter me! What would Noel do?!* she thought, only to notice Jarg now standing right in front of her.

"Oh blurf," Alex muttered as Jarg raised his mace. She tried to get her legs moving but to no avail. It was like she was living in a nightmare where the harder she tried to escape her foe, the more futile it became. "I'm so dead," she said before Jarg brought the spiked mace crashing down.

Alex thought she was done for, but in a blur, she found herself hovering above Jarg, her hands tightly grasped by her flying bestie.

"Are you okay?!" Sara grunted as she carried Alex several drux above Jarg. "I got worried when I saw you freeze up."

"I am, thanks to you!" Alex exclaimed with a sigh of relief as she found herself capable of moving once more. "Jarg nearly had me there."

"I told you we should have just left! Trying to help Ricky is going to get us killed!"

"I know. But we can't leave Ricky, Sara. Mr. Striker said that he was a part of our group. That means whether we like it or not, we can't leave him behind."

"...I still don't think he's worth the hassle," Sara muttered before resuming to speak. "So, what's the plan? Chuck was doable, but this monster underneath us is a whole different breed, Alex. We need some kind of plan if we're to make it out of this alive."

"If only we could fight him without freezing up. My muscles just lock up every time I look at Jarg," Alex said with a shudder. "I don't know how you're able to move right now, Sara."

"Just don't look him in the eyes," Sara said, her face dark as she kept her sight far from the monster below them. "Back in Striker's classroom, Ricky said something about Jarg's glare being able to paralyze others. As long as we avoid looking at his face, we should be fine."

"I think we have more to worry about than his ugly face," Alex said, her eyes widening. Her body tensed up as she pointed downwards at Jarg as the monster lifted his mace overhead.

Jarg hurled his mace with deadly precision at the two girls while they hovered overhead. It whizzed towards them with the intensity and force of a raging cannonball. With a grunt, Sara narrowly avoided the mace. It crashed into the ceiling with a loud CRACK. Alex looked with disbelief at the new crater in the ceiling that was several times bigger than the one she had created. The only small source of consolation she found was that Jarg's mace was now firmly planted in the center of the cavity and now out of their foe's reach.

"That smashing stick packs more of a punch than my sister's fists. There is no way that we can face Jarg head-on. Can you grab both me and Ricky and just fly us out?" Alex asked, only for Sara to shake her head.

"Carrying just one person puts an enormous strain on my ponytail," Sara grunted. "Carrying two people is out of the question. Besides, even if I could, there is no way we could go fast enough to escape Jarg. We need a plan and fast!"

"At least Jarg's only weapon is stuck on the ceiling. He won't be able to get us now."

"I wouldn't be so sure, Alex," Sara said while pointing upwards with Alex's gaze following until it fell on Jarg's mace. Her eyes widened at the sight of the mace rattling violently until it shot out of the ceiling and zoomed back into Jarg's outstretched hand.

"No way!" Alex screamed. "He can summon it back to his hand?!"

"You better believe it, Alex!" Ricky bellowed with a smug expression. "Jarg's mace is enchanted with dark power. It travels back to him with the same intensity that he lobs it. Does Noel or Officer Bryan have a weapon even remotely as cool?!"

Before anyone could respond, Jarg threw his mace again. It flew like a vulture of death with its sight set on the two girls.

"Sara, look out!!!" Alex screamed. "The stick is heading straight towards us again!!! It's going to hit us!!!"

"I'd like to see it try!" Sara yelled with a tense smile, her eyes brimming with both determination and fear as the mace quickly closed the gap. Sara grunted loudly as she made a sharp turn, the mace missing her by a hair as it crashed into the ceiling once more, only to zoom back into Jarg's hand. Effortlessly, the monster continued to hurl his weapon at the girls with Sara continuously evading. After a few moments, Sara's velocity greatly decreased, sweat dripping from her whole body.

"Come on, Sara! Why are you and Alex continuing to flee?" Ricky taunted from behind Jarg. "I thought that you two wanted to save me from Jarg? Didn't you say that the things I summon are weak and not worth the time of day?"

"Shut up, Ricky," Sara yelled before turning to whisper to Alex, "We can't keep dodging this weapon forever. His mace is getting faster and stronger with every throw. I'm going to run out of steam soon if we don't do something."

"How about flying me to the ceiling again? I can make another rock fall with this one landing right on Jarg. That ought to take him out."

"That same lame strategy won't work on Jarg!" Ricky bellowed from below them. "Many strong warriors tried in vain to beat him and died horribly. He's a breed of monster way more powerful than Chuck! It'll take more than anything Mr. Striker taught you to win here!"

He has a point, Alex thought to herself with her eyes closed. *What would Noel do right now? Let's see...I remember her telling me, 'If you're ever up against someone you can't overpower, then hit them in their weak spot.'*

She scrunched her forehead and wrinkled her nose. Billowing smoke rose from her ears as her mind raced, trying to think of a plan. *Clearly, Sara and I can't overpower Jarg, so we need to hit his weak spot. But what weakness could this monster have? From what Ricky said before, this thing is an endless killing machine. What could possibly...* "I got it!" Alex exclaimed as a shadow fell over her. She heard a yelp and found herself plummeting before she could respond. She looked up to see Sara wide-eyed, her ponytail tangled around Jarg's mace as it hit the wall with a crash. Sara groaned loudly, the weight of her body held up solely by her long hair. With both hands, she tried to free her hair which was pinned in between Jarg's mace and the rocky wall, but found herself unable to free herself.

"Sara!" Alex yelled, managing to perform a somersault to break her fall as she landed on her feet.

"Alex, run!" Sara yelled with a horrified expression as she pointed in Alex's direction. "He's right behind you!"

Alex turned to see Jarg towering over her like an agent of death. He reeked of blood and destruction with this scent intensifying with every step closer. A sinister red light, that could be described as mesmerizing, beamed from behind the lenses of his mask. Without thinking, Alex looked deeply into this light as Jarg stepped within arm's reach of her. It felt like an intense, invisible force, binding her with fiery fingers. Her muscles went rigid and didn't want to move. Alex silently gasped for air; every breath was a struggle.

She stared in silent horror as Jarg stood before her with an outstretched hand. With a loud crack, the mace instantly returned to him, followed by the sound of Sara grunting as she fell to the rocky ground with a loud thud.

"W-why…are you…doing this?" Alex forced herself to ask.

Jarg didn't answer. His only response was slowly raising his mace overhead as he prepared the final blow.

"Not so tough now, are you, Alex," Ricky taunted with a malicious smile, his eyes gleaming with perverse delight. "You might be strong enough to crush rocks in your hands, but you're nothing compared to Jarg! I told you that he was an unstoppable force of death and destruction. Now our dear classmates will learn this firsthand as well!"

Jarg turned away from Alex and faced Ricky, perhaps just now realizing the presence of the boy. He cocked his head slightly while looking at Ricky with a curious glance as the boy's evil smile stretched across his face.

"Jarg, I command you to go to Battletown Elementary and slaughter everyone there! Make this entire cavern floor run red with their blood!" Ricky commanded while standing erect, his rat-like teeth visible as his tongue licked his lips. "Then emerge from the ground and demolish the proud and mighty folks who live on the surface!"

Jarg didn't move, choosing instead to keep staring eerily at Ricky.

"Jarg! Do as I say and destroy the children who have shunned and ridiculed me this instant! I command you to obey me!" Ricky exclaimed with a huffy look, pointing excessively in the direction of the school, but Jarg continued to stare at him motionlessly, much to the boy's ire. "Don't just stand there! Get moving, stupid!"

Jarg's head turned with a sharp movement. With heavy steps, the monster trudged towards Ricky. The ground trembled as Jarg repeatedly struck the ground with his mace. Ricky's arrogant expression transformed into one of bewilderment as Jarg slowly stepped closer and closer. In a moment, Ricky's eyes widened in horror as he swiftly kept his line of vision downcast as Jarg's crimson glare bathed over him, causing him to shiver.

"Jarg, s-stop! What are you doing?! I'm on your side!" Ricky screamed with a slight tremor in his voice as Jarg stepped within striking distance. With rat-like movements, Ricky tried to scurry away, but Jarg quickly grabbed him by the neck with his free hand. Ricky tried to scream as he felt the powerful fingers crushing his windpipe, but he could barely utter a pained squeal. Effortlessly, Jarg turned Ricky around until the now terrified boy was facing him. Ricky's body went rigid and shook violently as the boy tried desperately to flee, but his muscles refused to cooperate under the intense influence of Jarg's menacing stare.

Much to everyone's surprise, Jarg set his mace down on the ground. Then he reached for his mask and slowly lifted it. The hair on the back of Ricky's neck stood up and his knees nearly buckled with terror. Under the mask was a dark abyss surrounded by several sharp teeth. Within the dark pit was a piercing, red eye that glowed menacingly.

"No!!! Please, Jarg, spare me!!! I worship you!!!" Ricky screamed, his voice raspy. His eyes filled with tears and he began whimpering hysterically while begging for mercy. He could feel his body growing cold as if that red eye sucked the warmth right out of his bones.

But the creature heard none of it. A deafening roar from Jarg's facial void filled the air. Ricky felt a powerful, invisible force pulling at him, pulling him toward the void. His skin shook from the powerful suction, and his whole body slowly slid closer to Jarg.

"But you're my hero!" Ricky whimpered, struggling with all of his might to escape, but to no avail. Ricky slid closer and closer to the dark, bottomless void and the piercing red eye that stared at him hungrily.

"You're not getting Ricky today!" Alex yelled as she leaped up, and with a mighty spinning aerial attack, kicked Jarg's red eye. The creature groaned as he stumbled backwards and released its hold on Ricky. The shocked boy fell to the ground with a yelp while clutching his throat. Without wasting a moment, Alex dashed towards Ricky and grabbed his hands before yanking him up to his feet. "Come, Ricky! We have to run!"

"How did you do that, Alex?" Ricky muttered; his eyes filled with awe as he gazed at Alex, who flashed him a big smile in return. Before Alex could respond, Jarg recovered and quickly picked up it's mace and trudged towards Alex and Ricky. Noticing Jarg's swift approach, Alex quickly pulled out another rock from her pocket and hurled it with impressive force as it zoomed through the air and crashed into Jarg's eye. The creature groaned, clutching at it's face as it stumbled backwards several steps.

During the creature's momentary daze, Alex grabbed Ricky's wrist and quickly bolted away from Jarg while half-dragging her comrade behind her.

"Well, Noel told me that if you can't find someone's weak spot, attack either their face, stomach, or groin," she said proudly as she puffed out her chest. "I almost went for the groin kick, but when I saw that X on Jarg's mask, I thought that it was a marker on where to attack."

"I'm not talking about Jarg's weak spot, Alex," Ricky sighed before shaking his head. "What I meant was how did you find the strength to attack Jarg? Just being around him frightens most into a state of paralysis before he quickly ends them. Why would you risk your life for me? I'm not even your friend; I'm just the kid nobody likes."

"Don't be stupid, Ricky! I don't want you dead!" Alex ex-claimed; her grip tightened as she turned to look at him with fierce eyes. "You're still a part of my team and I will do every-thing I can to protect you from anything that crosses our path! Whether we're facing one Jarg or ten, I'll kick each and every one of them in their faces however many times it takes to keep you safe from harm!"

For once, Ricky was speechless. Alex saw the boy she disliked choke up and tear up slightly. She turned her head back to what was ahead of her while Ricky wiped at his eyes. After a moment, she heard Ricky mutter a single "Thank you," under his breath. A small smile formed on Alex's face as she gave Ricky's fingers a gentle squeeze.

It was a low groan that caught Alex's attention. She turned towards the groaning and saw her fallen bestie lying flat on her back upon the cold cavern floor. Increasing her pace, Alex dashed towards her best friend and didn't stop until both she and Ricky reached the spot where Sara lay.

"Sara, wake up!" Alex screamed as she grabbed her friend's shoulders and quickly shook her. "We have to get out of here now!"

"Uuugggh," Sara groaned as her eyes slowly fluttered open. "That mace really packs a wallop. I think I'm seeing stars right now, Alex."

"Can you still fly?" Alex asked while helping pull Sara up to her feet. Her friend was more than a little wobbly, swaying from side to side with a dazed expression.

"I can in a bit, but not for much longer," Sara whined while clutching her ponytail tenderly. "My roots are aching."

"Your hair is the least of our troubles," Ricky muttered. "Right now we have one of the most dangerous serial killers ever to deal with."

"And whose fault is that, Rat Face?!" Sara grumbled, giving Ricky a piercing glare. "Your stupid obsession with monsters is the only reason that we're even in this mess! How about you make yourself useful and tell us how to beat this thing!"

"Are you crazy, Sara?" Ricky mumbled with a hopeless expression. "No one can stop Jarg when he's on a rampage."

"I don't know how, Ricky," Alex said with a determined expression as Jarg pulled his mask over his face and trudged towards them with mace in hand. "But somehow, we're going to do just that."

Chapter 7- Battle with a Real Monster Part 2

The light from Jarg's eye bathed the three children, beckoning them to meet its stare. They kept their eyes downcast to avoid meeting Jarg's gaze as his heavy steps grew closer. Looking at the monster's shadow, they saw him raise his mace overhead, preparing to strike them down.

"Run, guys!" Alex yelled as they quickly scattered before Jarg's mace hit the ground, barely missing the children.

"That was too close!" Sara screamed, her ponytail, now covered in dirt and grime, swaying in rhythm with her rapid footsteps trying to outrun the lumbering monster trailing behind her on the unlevel ground. The sound of Jarg's heavy steps chasing after her in hot pursuit was unnerving. Despite her best efforts, she couldn't shake Jarg. She briefly glanced back, and out of the corner of her eye, was horrified to see that the behemoth was gradually catching up to her. "How the blurf is he catching up to me?!! I'm not looking at that thing's face and I still feel like I'm moving slower than normal!"

"That's Jarg's monstrous presence!" Ricky exclaimed. "His bloodlust is so strong that it slows down nearby weaker prey."

"Good to know, Ricky!" Sara yelled back, trying to focus on her footwork on the dark, rocky ground. "Can you tell us how to stop it?!"

"You don't! The best you can do is try to avoid his mace!"

"Easier said than done!" Sara barked after ducking her head to avoid the swing of Jarg's mace. "This thing isn't making it easy!"

"Then just fly already, helicopter head!" Ricky barked back.

"You think I'd still be running on foot if I could? My roots still need a little longer to cool off before I can fly again!" Sara hissed at him, turning her face to give him a piercing glare, and in the process, taking her focus away from where her feet landed.

"AAAAAHHH!" Sara screamed, her foot hitting a gaping pothole that sent her sprawling forward. She tumbled haphazardly for a moment until she found herself flat on her back, with several scrapes on her body. When she opened her eyes, everything was blurred and spinning. When her vision cleared, the only sight to greet her was that of Jarg raising his mace to snuff out the rest of her life.

"Not today, Jarg!" Alex screamed while soaring in the air over Sara, her foot hurtling at an intense speed as it collided with Jarg's mask. The monster groaned lowly as it stumbled backward a few steps. Alex quickly dashed towards Sara and helped pull her to her feet. "Are you okay?"

"Yes...just a few scrapes and bruises. If it wasn't for you, then I'd be a bloody pancake now."

"Happy to help—" Alex said before a hand with an iron-clad grip grabbed her and pinned her to the ground. The bewildered girl struggled to break free, but that ceased instantly when her eyes accidently met the red light coming from behind Jarg's mask.

"Alex, NO!!!" Sara yelled, but before she could do anything, Jarg turned to meet her gaze, and now with both girls frozen, he raised his mace once more to finish them. Before he could deliver that final finisher, the soft scrape of tiny, clawed feet filled the air. In an instant, Jarg found himself covered in several rats that tore at his clothes and bit him. The monster turned away, ripping the creatures off his grotesque body with the sound of many high-pitched squeals ending abruptly as Jarg squeezed the life out of every rat that he could grab.

"That ought to keep him distracted for a moment, you two. Now run!" Ricky yelled with both palms opened as several more rats appeared within them only to hop off and scurry towards Jarg.

"Thanks, Ricky!" Alex exclaimed with a smile before grabbing Sara's hand and pulling her towards Ricky. "We'd be dead right now without you."

Ricky turned away, trying to hide a small, bashful smile.

"He's also the reason we're here in the first place, Alex," Sara grumbled.

Ricky's smile quickly transformed into a snarl. "Oh yeah, well you're just a—" Ricky started before being interrupted by Alex.

"Ricky, now isn't the time. We need to do something if we're to walk out of this room alive. You know more about Jarg than us. He must have some kind of weakness that we can use against him. How was Jarg defeated before?"

"Ancient warriors from this realm channeled the power of their God through light to defeat him. Jarg is a monster of the night with light counteracting his strength," Ricky said grimly. "In this underground cavern, he's at full strength without a way to fatally harm him."

"Well, we'll just have to think of something," Alex said before a rock fell on her head. "Ouch!"

She rubbed the top of her head tenderly before looking up at the cracked and crumbling ceiling above them, revealing a single ray of light. A smile stretched her face as a crazy idea formed.

"Ricky, can your rats climb the walls?" Alex asked.

"Sure, but why do you ask—" He started before noticing the damaged ceiling. "You can't be serious, Alex!"

"I'm afraid she's very serious, Ricky," Sara said with a sigh. She slapped his back before pushing him forward. "You best get those rodents moving, Rat Face. We'll provide you cover."

"Whatever," Ricky mumbled before sticking his hand in his mouth and whistling sharply. Every nearby rat immediately perked up their head and looked up at Ricky pointing towards the ceiling. Obediently, the remaining rats leaped off of Jarg. They scurried up the walls and began chewing at the ceiling.

"Rats are so gross," Sara muttered before turning towards Alex. "Besties Trapeze?"

"Let's pester this monster," Alex said after grabbing Sara's hands. "Like flies on a corpse! Let's fly, Sara!"

With a low hum, Sara's ponytail spun like a powerful propeller with both girls instantly hovering off the ground and zooming up above Jarg. They circled around the monster with Sara swinging Alex around like a pendulum.

"Come and get me, you blurfing monster!" Alex yelled as she released her grip on Sara and soared like a dove. With deadly precision, Jarg threw his mace at Alex, but before it could connect, Sara swooped in and pulled Alex out of its path. The ceiling shook violently as the mace crashed into it, causing the cracks on the ceiling to widen with several chunks of rock breaking off. Ricky's rats squeaked, a few falling from the ceiling. Those who remained steadfastly attached kept diligently scratching and biting at the damaged ceiling around a drux radius of Jarg's mace.

It didn't stay planted on the ceiling for long. Jarg quickly outstretched his arm with the mace breaking free and swiftly returning back to Jarg's hand. Tirelessly, Jarg kept aiming at Alex as Sara continuously kept launching Alex up in the air only for Sara to pull Alex out of harm's way whenever the mace would get too close. However, Sara and Alex's movements gradually slowed while Jarg showed no signs of fatigue.

"Ricky, how's it coming along?!" Alex yelled in between heavy pants.

"Not very well!" he said with a shake of his head while pointing to the damaged ceiling. The brown, rocky outer layer had been broken through, revealing a thick layer of black, crystalized stone. "My rats have hit a layer of obsidian ziglinite! The stuff is harder to break through than even the regular ones we had in Mr. Striker's classroom! It'll probably take my rats at least a few more yosmins to finish!"

"Maybe we can finish this quickly if we can get Jarg's mace to hit the ceiling one more time," Alex said when out of the corner of her eye she saw Jarg's mace zooming towards them. "Sara, look out! It's coming fast from the rear on your right!"

With a nod, Sara swiftly flew out of the mace's path. Her eyes widened, though, when it suddenly span. The heavy shaft slammed into her stomach, leaving her gasping for air. She released her hold on Alex, both girls plummeting towards the ground.

This is going to hurt, Alex thought as both she and Sara closed their eyes. It was much to their surprise when their descent stopped abruptly. Their feet dangled helplessly in the air with an intense pressure gripping their necks. With horrified expressions, they opened their eyes and found themselves looking into Jarg's mask. Both girls wanted to scream but could not utter a sound. They struggled to break free from this monster's ensnaring red light, but their bodies refused to cooperate, and even if they did, it would take a miracle to break free from his monstrous grip.

"Let them go!" Ricky yelled as he opened up his palm with two more rats appearing within them. However, before he could utter a word, Jarg hurled both girls right at him. Ricky grunted from the impact of the two girls and fell to the ground with both Alex and Sara on top of him. "Ow! Will you two get off!" he yelled, only for his face to go pale and his muscles to tense up when he saw Jarg standing above them. Both girls followed his gaze and instantly felt their arms and legs freeze up.

Jarg raised his arm, his mace returning to his hand as he lifted his mask, revealing his dark void of a face. A powerful suction came from the void, beckoning the three to venture into the darkness with cold fingers tirelessly tugging at their flesh. Slowly, bit by bit, they found themselves being dragged closer to the place devoid of light and eternally cold.

Noel, please save me. I'm so scared right now, Alex thought desperately as she was pulled closer to the void.

It was the loud cracking and crumbling of the ceiling that caused everyone, even Jarg, to look up as a barrage of jagged rocks splintered off from the ceiling and came crashing down. Rays of light pierced the darkness of the cavern with the accompaniment of the loud squeals of a multitude of rats raining from the now huge, gaping hole above them. Alex, Sara, and Ricky quickly jumped up and dashed away from the falling rocks as they hit the ground with loud crashes. Only Jarg stood still. He uttered no sound and showed no fear before many giant boulders crashed into him in a deadly embrace.

After a few moments, there was silence once more. The three children stood silently with shock, trying to process everything that just happened as they stared at the now bright sunlight filling the cavern. After a moment, a huge smile formed on both Alex and Sara's faces at the sight of the pile of large rocks that covered the cavern floor.

"We did it!" Alex and Sara exclaimed while jumping up and high-fiving in midair.

Meanwhile, Ricky stared at the scene, mouth agape. "How are we not dead?"

"Because Jarg's got nothing on us!" Sara boasted pridefully with her hands on her hips. "And now we sent his sorry butt to the Den of the Defeated."

Both she and Alex leaped up on the closest rock and began crawling up the pile until they were at the very top. Gleefully, they both danced with silly movements upon the accumulation of boulders as Ricky watched the rocks keenly, his body rigid and ready to flee.

"Alex, Sara," Ricky said with a fearful expression, "Jarg's not dead."

Both girls' dancing ceased immediately.

"What are you talking about? He's buried under a huge pile of rocks," Alex said while motioning towards the boulders below her and Sara's feet.

"Jarg is a creature of darkness. Only light can destroy him," he said as the pile of rocks began to shake. "Quick, get down!" he yelled as all of the rocks in the pile instantly shot around the room. Alex and Sara fell to the ground with shocked expressions, grunting after landing on their bottoms. They groaned until they looked up and noticed Jarg standing right before them. He was covered in deep scrapes, with a thick, black liquid seeping out. A dark smoke came from the parts of his body exposed to the sunlight with his skin quickly blackening. That didn't faze him as he trudged towards them with his mace held high.

The three kids could only watch in horror as this monster approached them with intense bloodlust.

"That's enough, foul beast!!!" a voice called out from beyond the gaping hole in the ceiling.

A flash of gold and crimson leaped from the hole and landed directly between the kids and Jarg. Much to their relief, they saw standing before them a flowing royal-red cape with bright yellow trim attached to a familiar figure clad in striking samurai armor.

"When I heard the loud crashing, I thought that a flock of three-headed chickens were rampaging the underground caverns again, but this is a mess far different than what I anticipated. I told you three to stay off of the Crimson Path," Mr. Striker said with a disappointed tone after glancing at Alex, Sara, and Ricky before focusing his gaze on Jarg. "You three have been playing with dark forces beyond your control. Stay behind me; I'll deal with this creature."

His crimson eyes burned with a fire-like intensity. Several humongous, blazing, red swords instantly appeared and began circling around him. He grunted a few words that the kids couldn't make out. The swords flashed in response and moved away from Mr. Striker. Two of the flaming weapons hovered in front of the three children in a defensive stance with the remaining swords forming a giant circle around Mr. Striker and the looming monster before him.

Jarg turned his head to look at the nearby swords. They pierced the rocky ground around him, leaving much of it scorched. He swung his mace at one of the blazing swords. His mace effortlessly passed through, but it was now covered in flames. The obsidian smoke coming off of his body thickened as his exposed flesh became ash-like. Alarmed, Jarg wildly struck the ground with his mace, causing the rocky terrain to shake, but the fire stubbornly clung to the malicious mace. Uttering a low growl while holding his mace far from his mask, he slowly turned towards Mr. Striker.

Mr. Striker unsheathed his gleaming crimson blade and held it up with the blade pointing towards Jarg. The monster's advance halted briefly; his posture tightened. Jarg's focus shifted entirely to Mr. Striker's katana. After a brief standoff, Jarg gripped his mace with both hands and dashed towards Mr. Striker with a threatening roar.

"Creature of darkness," Mr. Striker uttered before raising his katana and sprinting towards Jarg with an intense burst of speed. "Begone! Now taste my crimson blade!" he yelled as he brought down his weapon. The crimson metal slashed through Jarg from top to bottom with the welder's mask falling to the burnt ground. The dark void of Jarg's face split in two as it was bathed by the sun's bright light. The bottomless shadows quickly disappeared from Jarg's split head with his whole body turning to a pile of soot after being bathed in the intense rays of light.

"May your soul find rest in the Den," Mr. Striker muttered respectfully before flicking the black blood off of his katana and sheathing his blade. The flames from his conjured swords dissipated in a dazzling display of embers which left all three kids slack-jawed and with gleaming wide eyes.

"Mr. Striker, you're so cool!" all three kids exclaimed as they hovered around their teacher with joyful expressions.

"We'll see if you three still think that after spending time in the poison-spewing petunia patch with concrete slabs resting on your knees," he said sternly with his arms crossed. "What could have possibly led you all to think that summoning some murderous monster was a good idea?"

"Well...um..." Alex and Sara stuttered before Ricky interrupted them.

"It was my idea, sir," Ricky said with a remorseful expression, his face downcast. Both girls were shocked as he stepped in front of them and put a hand over his heart. "I made a bet with them that Jarg could defeat them in a fight, so I brought them down here and performed the ritual that summoned Jarg. It's my fault that we were put in peril today."

"Ricky," Mr. Striker said harshly with his eyes narrowed. "I cannot emphasize enough just how serious this matter is. What you did here today was incredibly foolish. You put not just your life at risk, but also Alex, Sara, and everyone at Battletown Elementary. You know acts resulting in death carry massive consequences, Ricky, and if you had succeeded in unleashing Jarg on the school, you would been marked for death and ostracized from society, if Jarg didn't end your life first. Whatever could have possessed you to bring forth a creature like Jarg, knowing how grave the consequences are?"

"Because he was my hero," Ricky muttered, his eyes downcast and unable to meet his teacher's gaze. "He's strong and can easily kill his foes. He never has to be afraid of others because everyone else is terrified of him."

"Ricky," Mr. Striker said, "Jarg is a monster, not a hero. Heroes help others and inspire them to do the same. All monsters do is steal, kill, and destroy."

"There are no heroes in my life, Mr. Striker," Ricky grumbled bitterly. "The only thing I have left to turn to are monsters."

"Then your next assignment is to find a hero," Mr. Striker said as he bent down and put a hand on Ricky's shoulder. "Someone who leaves a positive impact on those around him or her and to learn from them. I want a ten-page essay turned in to me by the end of the week. In the meantime, I will be meeting with Principal Freuaget and the rest of the school board to discuss the situation more thoroughly, and to determine an appropriate punishment for your actions against this school and its student body."

Ricky sighed. "Yes, sir."

"Good. Now, you two," Mr. Striker said, turning to face Alex and Sara. "You two are in hot water as well. You two knew that the Crimson Path was forbidden and you both still chose to go down it. I'm disappointed in both of you."

Alex and Sara's faces became downcast, but they were startled when they felt his hands firmly grasp their shoulders.

"Despite the dangers you two faced, you fought valiantly and even worked together with Ricky. I'd say that you passed my lesson with flying colors. Both Noel and Officer Bryan would be so proud of you two. Here, take this," he said, handing them both a sticker with a smiling, crimson flame that read 'You're on fire!'

"Sweet! This is great!" Alex exclaimed, quickly putting the sticker on her shirt.

"Don't get too carried away, you two. I'm still expecting a ten-page essay from both of you about this incident and what you've learned as a result."

"I thought you were going to say that," Sara grumbled before glancing at the sticker and giving a half smile. "At least this sticker is cute."

"Now, let's head back to the school, you three. You are already late for your next class, Follow me. I'll lead you back the right way," Mr. Striker said as he turned and began walking down the dark pathway before halting; his narrowed eyes taking note of the children's dirt-covered clothes. "but first, let's get you three cleaned up. I won't allow any of you to track dirt inside the school after the floors were just swept."

Mr. Striker took a deep breath before shooting a powerful burst of air from his mouth which blasted the kids. Alex, Sara, and Ricky looked down at their messy clothes in awe as their teacher's focused breath blew every last spec of filth off them leaving them cleaner.

"Alright, now let's head back." He said motioning to them as he resumed to briskly walk down the path.

Sara and Ricky immediately followed after him, but Alex stayed in place for a moment. Mr. Striker, noticing the deep look in her eyes, faced her and asked, "Is there something wrong, Alex?"

"Mr. Striker, did you do away with Jarg forever?"

Mr. Striker paused for a moment before responding. "True evil is never completely done away with in this world. Monsters like Jarg tend to linger in the shadows lying in wait. Evil of that multitude can't be fought alone, but it always crumbles when it is confronted by a gathering of people choosing to be a bright light for those trapped in the shadows. Honesty, I hope that we never run into the likes of Jarg again."

"Me too!" Alex said with a big smile on her face. "I've had plenty of fun fighting serial killers, but it'll be nice not having head-smashing monsters chasing after us."

"You said it!" Sara beamed with a tired smile. She put her arm on Alex's neck. "It'll be nice to be back in class."

"Yeah, it'll be history period next," Rick muttered, his skin still a little pale, but his eyes gleamed as a big smile covered his face. "I can't wait to hear more about three-headed chickens and the impact they had during the time of our founding fathers. Um...if you two want, then maybe..."

"Yeah, I'm not interested in any of that," Sara muttered under her breath while rolling her eyes. She gave Alex the symbol to shut down Ricky, but to her surprise, Alex smiled at him.

"I think that meeting up with you would be a great idea," Alex said matter-of-factly. "History is one of our weaker subjects; maybe you can help tutor us?"

"Only if you two can help me out with rock crushing. I'm still not doing good with that."

"You got it, pal," Alex said as she put an arm around Ricky's neck and began pulling him towards the exit. Slowly, all four Sidvans disappeared in the shadows as they made their way back to school, but before they were gone, Alex's voice could be heard one last time. "You'll have a grip stronger than Jarg's once I'm done with you."

| 90 | –   CHAPTER 7- BATTLE WITH A REAL MONSTER
PART 2

Epilogue

"**M**an, what a day," a woman in her early twenties with a brown, braided ponytail grumbled. The sleeves of her white button-up shirt were rolled up to her elbows as she tightly gripped a familiar katana with a shiny, crimson blade. She raised the weapon over her head and took a deep breath before bringing the blade down. With a deft motion, the blade easily sliced through the block of orange cheese sitting on a black cutting board with the dairy product quickly reduced to several thick slices.

"That's what I'm talking about!" the woman exclaimed with an excited gleam in her eyes as she quickly sheathed the sword and leaned it against her desk before taking a seat at it. She opened a plastic wrapper of salted crackers and began stacking slices of cheese onto them. After eating a few, she slumped against her desk; her face pressed against the white, marbled counter right next to the nameplate that read 'Ms. Jilper' in blue letters. "I may need to take a nap. That cheese is a lot more bitter than I thought."

Her mind wandered to the icy mountains of a far-off country, only to stop abruptly when she heard the pattering of several little paws scurrying around the floor. Still drowsy, she slowly opened one eye but saw nothing out of the ordinary on the ground.

"I must be losing it. Teaching these kids is starting to get to me," she muttered sleepily as her classroom door opened. With metallic steps, a figure she was very familiar with stepped into the room.

"That PTA meeting regarding the recent outbreak of rumble bees and three-headed chickens ran later than I thought it would. Did you save me any cheese crackers, Jan?" Mr. Striker asked as he approached with a fat stack of papers in his hands that he quickly placed on her desk. "Remind me again why you needed my katana to cut your cheese instead of using one of your many elegant kitchen knives?"

"Because this is no ordinary cheese, Kusanagi," Jan said, looking up with a small smile. "This is my grandmother's super-secret recipe for insanely sharp, soul-shredding, cheddar cheese. Only the most well-honed blades can slash through it, and with this batch in particular, I felt like only your katana could do the job."

"Is that so?" Mr. Striker chuckled as he pulled up a chair and sat across from Jan. His red eyes, full of a tender warmth, looked deeply into her blue irises. "How'd my blade fare against your grandmother's cheese?"

"Oh, it was a knockout!" she exclaimed excitedly before a sudden realization dawned upon her, causing her muscles to ache and her head to hurt. With a frustrated expression, she quickly buried her face in her arms on the desk and turned away from Mr. Striker with a loud groan.

"Why the long face?" He reached for her hand and gave it a gentle squeeze. "It's unlike you to be so melancholy, especially after getting to snack on your grandmother's famous cheese. Is the cheese bandit at it again?"

"No, it's just been one of those days today, you know, Kusanagi," Jan sighed as she slowly sat straight up; her brown bangs fell over her eyes. She removed her hand from Mr. Striker's grip as she grasped her forehead and groaned. "I put Noel in detention this afternoon for several rude remarks she made to me in class."

"You let her off easier than I would have," he said with another chuckle as he softly rearranged her bangs out of her eyes before a scary gleam filled his flaming pupils. "I would have had her kneeling for hours with several slabs of concrete resting on her thighs. I can't stand disorderly conduct."

"Maybe I should take a page out of your book then," she replied with a laugh. "She is so disrespectful. It's driving me up the walls. How is it with her little sister?"

"Alex? She's a precious gem. Unlike her sister, she's kind-hearted, acrobatic like a wild monkey, and works very well with others."

"She sounds way better than Noel. Do you want to trade?"

"You'll get your turn soon enough," Mr. Striker said with a smirk. "Besides, she has a bit of a mischievous side as well. You heard about the trouble she got into a few days ago?"

"I did. I'm glad you were there to intervene. Jarg's reputation must have been greatly exaggerated with how easily he was dealt with."

"We're fortunate I found him early after he had been summoned before he could start devouring souls. If we had been a day later confronting him, his strength would be far greater than what I could have handled even with Momaka Makamo. Speaking of which, where is my katana?"

"Don't you see it? I left it right here—" Jan said, pointing to where she had rested the sword, only for her expression to become confused when she saw that the katana was no longer there. "Wait! Where did it go?! I just set it down there a moment ago!" Jan exclaimed as she leaped out of her chair and quickly examined the area around the desk. "Someone must have taken it while I was napping, but who?"

"I think I know who took my katana," Mr. Striker said in a controlled tone, noticing something on the floor. He quickly picked it up and brought it up to his face.

"What's that?" Jan asked.

"Rat's hair," Mr. Striker muttered, his crimson eyes blazing intensely as he stood and stormed out of Jan's classroom. "Looks like I'll be using my concrete slabs today during detention!"

...

It was a quiet day in the caverns...much too quiet. The only sound was the soft scurry of steps scampering against the rock-hard ground.

"Finally," Ricky said with a serious expression while sauntering down the underground caverns. It was dark and bone-chilling, yet he kept marching forward with a determined look in his eyes. Mr. Striker's katana clanged noisily within its sheath as he made his way down the Crimson Path. "Now that I have Mr. Striker's sword, I should have more than enough strength to do what needs to be done."

After a while of navigating, he found himself standing before a familiar black altar. He quickly ripped the sheath off of the katana and threw it to the ground before pointing the blade towards the black altar. "Take this!" he yelled as he dashed towards the altar and took a heavy swing at it. The sword hit it with a loud clang. "Ouch!" Ricky yelled. The katana rattled strongly until it shook itself out of his grip. It fell to the ground with a ring while Ricky blew on his fingers.

"That altar must be made out of something really strong." he moaned. "Then maybe I should change my approach."

Ricky reached into his pocket and pulled out a vial filled with a green liquid. After uncapping it, he splashed the plasma around the altar and began chanting in a low voice.

"Now, Jarg, I summon you back into this world!" Ricky yelled before a dark hole appeared in front of him. Slowly, the towering figure wearing a welder's mask rose out of the void. Within his right hand, he tightly clutched his spiked stone mace.

"You're just as terrifying as before," Ricky muttered under his breath while avoiding eye contact with the monster before him. "But I'm not scared of you this time. I'm your master,

Jarg, and as the one who summoned you, I command you to do my bidding! Now destroy this altar, Jarg!"

The monster faced him but refused to budge.

"It seems that I will need to show you who's boss, then," he said as he bent his knees and quickly grabbed the fallen katana. Ricky tightly gripped the hilt of the sword and pointed the shining blade towards Jarg. "Now it's time for me to prove my strength by making mincemeat of you! Today will be the day I prove myself to Alex!" he yelled as he dashed towards Jarg with sword raised. With a swift slash, his sword made a diagonal cut in Jarg's chest that ran through his stomach.

The monster didn't flinch.

Before Ricky could safely land, Jarg swung his mace into Ricky's abdomen. With quick reflexes, Ricky brought up his sword, the hilt taking the brunt of the blow. The katana shot out of his grip with Ricky flying into the cavern's back wall with a loud crack.

"Owww," Ricky groaned as he fell to the ground with a thud. He rubbed his back tenderly. His vision was blurred, and when it finally cleared, all he saw was Jarg standing in front of him. His muscles froze. It was a struggle just to gasp for air as Jarg slowly raised his mace overhead to strike.

"Oh rat poop," he muttered helplessly as Jarg brought his mace down.

Nobutaro Masai is the author of Battletown Tales 1 Rocks, Rats, & Role Models and Knockout Noel. He lives in Pensacola, Florida with his dogs Indy, Kakashi, and Zero. He enjoys video games and anime, spending time with friends and family, writing stories, and looks forward to the day where he can exchange marital vows with his beautiful fiance, Brittany, and live happily ever after.

www.ingramcontent.com/pod-product-compliance
Lightning Source LLC
Chambersburg PA
CBHW070449170726
48291CB00005B/1663